What others have said about *The Cabala*:

"Mr. Wilder is a fine stylist; he clothes his mysticism in his style and lightens it with jewels of charming observation and felicitous expression."

—*The New York Times*

". . . the fascinating characters frequently galvanize the story into brilliant life . . ."

—*Saturday Review of Literature*

"Mr. Wilder's prose is exceptionally beautiful; its texture has a rare consistence of distinctive weaving."

—*Literary Review*

# THORNTON WILDER

# THE CABALA

Carroll & Graf Publishers, Inc.
New York

Copyright © 1926 by Albert & Charles Boni
Copyright renewed 1954 by Thornton Wilder.

Published by arrangement with Harper & Row Publishers, Inc.

First Carroll & Graf edition 1987

Carroll & Graf Publishers, Inc.
260 Fifth Avenue
New York, New York 10001

ISBN: 0-88184-295-8

Manufactured in the United States of America

To my friends at the American Academy
in Rome, 1920-1921
T.W.

# CONTENTS

# THE
# CABALA

# BOOK ONE

---

# FIRST ENCOUNTERS

The train that first carried me into Rome was late, overcrowded and cold. There had been several unexplained waits in an open field, and midnight found us still moving slowly across the Campagna toward the faintly-colored clouds that hung above Rome. At intervals we stopped at platforms where flaring lamps lit up for a moment some splendid weather-moulded head. Darkness surrounded these platforms, save for glimpses of a road and the dim outlines of a mountain ridge. It was Virgil's country and there was a wind that seemed to rise from the fields and descend upon us in a long Virgilian sigh, for the land that has inspired sentiment in the poet ultimately receives its sentiment from him.

The train was overcrowded, because some tourists had discovered on the previous day that the beggars of Naples smelt of carbolic acid. They concluded at once that the authorities had struck a case or two of

1

Indian cholera and were disinfecting the underworld by a system of enforced baths. The air of Naples generates legend. In the sudden exodus tickets for Rome became all but improcurable, and First Class tourists rode Third, and interesting people rode First.

In the carriage it was cold. We sat in our overcoats meditating, our eyes glazed by resignation or the glare. In one compartment a party drawn from that race that travels most and derives least pleasure from it, talked tirelessly of bad hotels, the ladies sitting with their skirts whipped about their ankles to discourage the ascent of fleas. Opposite them sprawled three American Italians returning to their homes in some Apennine village after twenty years of trade in fruit and jewelry on upper Broadway. They had invested their savings in the diamonds on their fingers, and their eyes were not less bright with anticipation of a family reunion. One foresaw their parents staring at them, unable to understand the change whereby their sons had lost the charm the Italian soil bestows upon the humblest of its children, noting only that they have come back with bulbous features, employing barbarous idioms and bereft forever of the witty psychological intuition of their race. Ahead of them lay some sleepless bewildered nights above their mothers' soil floors and muttering poultry.

In another compartment an adventuress in silver sables leaned one cheek against the shuddering windowpane. Opposite her a glittering-eyed matron stared with challenging persistency, ready to intercept any glance the girl might cast upon her dozing husband. In the corridor two young army officers lolled and preened and angled for her glance, like those insects in certain beautiful pages of Fabre, who go through the ritual of flirtation under futile condi-

2

tions, before a stone, merely because some associative motors have been touched.

There was a Jesuit with his pupils, filling the time with Latin conversation; a Japanese diplomat reverently brooding over a postage-stamp collection; a Russian sculptor sombrely reading the bony structure of our heads; some Oxford students carefully dressed for tramping, but riding over the richest tramping country in Italy; the usual old woman with a hen and the usual young American, staring. Such a company as Rome receives ten times a day, and remains Rome.

My companion sat reading a trodden copy of the London *Times*, real estate offers, military promotions and all. James Blair after six years of classical studies at Harvard had been sent to Sicily as archaeological adviser to a motion picture company bent on transferring the body of Greek mythology to the screen. The company had failed and been dispersed, and Blair thereafter had roamed the Mediterranean, finding stray employment and filling immense notebooks with his observations and theories. His mind brimmed with speculation: as to the chemical composition of Raphael's pigments; as to the lighting conditions under which the sculptors of antiquity wished their work to be viewed; as to the date of the most inaccessible mosaics in Santa Maria Maggiore. Of all these suggestions and many more he allowed me to make notes, even to the extent of copying some diagrams in colored inks. In the event of his being lost at sea with all his notebooks—a not improbable one, as he crosses the Atlantic on obscure and economical craft, not mentioned in your paper, even when they founder—it would be my confusing duty to make a gift of this material to the Librarian of Harvard University

3

where its unintelligibility might confer upon it an incomputable value.

Presently discarding his paper, Blair decided to talk: You may have come to Rome to study, but before you settle down to the ancients you see whether there aren't some interesting moderns.

There's no Ph.D. in modern Romans. Our posterity does that. What moderns do you mean?

Have you ever heard of the *Cabala?*

Which one?

A kind of a group living around Rome.

No.

They're very rich and influential. Everyone's afraid of them. Everybody suspects them of plots to overturn things.

Political?

No, not exactly. Sometimes.

Social swells?

Yes, of course. But more than that, too. Fierce intellectual snobs, they are. Mme. Agaropoulos is no end afraid of them. She says that every now and then they descend from Tivoli and intrigue some bill through the Senate, or some appointment in the Church, or drive some poor lady out of Rome.

Tchk!

It's because they're bored. Mme. Agaropoulos says they're frightfully bored. They've had everything so long. The chief thing about them is that they hate what's recent. They spend their time insulting new titles and new fortunes and new ideas. In lots of ways they're medieval. Just in their appearance for one thing. And in their ideas. I fancy it's like this: you've heard of scientists off Australia coming upon regions where the animals and plants ceased to evolve ages ago? They find a pocket of archaic time in the middle

4

of a world that has progressed beyond it. Well, it must be something like that with the Cabala. Here's a group of people losing sleep over a host of notions that the rest of the world has outgrown several centuries ago: one duchess' right to enter a door before another; the word order in a dogma of the Church; the divine right of kings, especially of Bourbons. They're still passionately in earnest about stuff that the rest of us regard as pretty antiquarian lore. What's more, these people that hug these notions aren't just hermits and ignored eccentrics, but members of a circle so powerful and exclusive that all these Romans refer to them with bated breath as the Cabala. They work with incredible subtlety, let me tell you, and have incredible resources in wealth and loyalty. I'm quoting Mme. Agaropoulos, who has a sort of hysterical fear of them, and thinks they're supernatural.

But she must know some of them personally.

Of course she does. So do I.

One isn't afraid of people one knows. Who's in it?

I'm taking you to meet one of them tomorrow, this Miss Grier. She's leader of the whole international set. I catalogued her library for her,—oh, I couldn't have got to know her any other way. I lived in her apartment in the Palazzo Barberini and used to get whiffs of the Cabala. Besides her there's a Cardinal. And the Princess d'Espoli who's mad. And Mme. Bernstein of the German banking family. Each one of them has some prodigious gift, and together they're miles above the next social stratum below them. They're so wonderful that they're lonely. I quote. They sit off there in Tivoli getting what comfort they can from one another's excellence.

5

Do they call themselves the Cabala. Are they organized?

Not as I see it. Probably it never occurred to them that they even constituted a group. I say, you study them up. You ferret it out, the whole secret. It's not my line.

In the pause that followed, fragments of conversation from the various corners of the compartment flowed in upon our minds so recently occupied with semi-divine personages. I haven't the slightest desire to quarrel, Hilda, muttered one of the Englishwomen. Naturally you made the arrangements for the trip as best you could. All I say is that that girl did *not* clean off the washstand every morning. There were rings and rings.

And from an American Italian: I says it's none of your goddam business, I says. Take your goddam shirt the hell outta here. He run, I tell you, he run so fast you don't see no dust for him he run so.

The Jesuit and his pupils had become politely interested in the postage stamps and the Japanese attaché was murmuring: Oh, most exclusively rare! The four-cent is pale violet and when held up to the light reveals a water-mark, a sea-horse. There are only seven in the world and three are in the collection of the Baron Rothschild.

Symphonically considered, one heard that there had been no sugar in it, that she had told Marietta three mornings running to put sugar in it, or bring sugar, although the Republic of Guatemala had immediately cut them, a few had leaked out to collectors, and that more musk-melons than one would have thought possible were sold annually at the corner of Broadway and 126th Street. Perhaps it was in revulsion against such small change that the impulse

6

first rose in me to pursue these Olympians, who though they might be bored and mistaken, had at least, each of them, "one prodigious gift."

It was in this company then, and in the dejected airs of one in the morning that I first arrived in Rome, in that station that is uglier than most, more hung with advertisements of medicinal waters and more redolent of ammonia. During the journey I had been planning what I should do the moment I arrived: fill myself with coffee and wine, and in the proud middle of the night, run down the Via Cavour. Under the hints of dawn I should behold the tribune of Santa Maria Maggiore, hovering above me like the ark on Ararat, and the ghost of Palestrina in a soiled cassock letting himself out at a side door and rushing home to a large family in five voices; hurry on to the platform before the Lateran where Dante mixes with the Jubilee crowd; overhang the Forum and skirt the locked Palatine; follow the river to the inn where Montaigne groans over his ailments; and fall a-staring at the Pope's cliff-like dwelling, where work Rome's greatest artists, the one who is never unhappy and the one who is never anything else. I would know my way about, for my mind is built upon the map of the city that throughout the eight years of school and college had hung above my desk, a city so longed for that it seemed as though in the depth of my heart I had never truly believed I should see it.

When I arrived finally, the station was deserted; there was no coffee, no wine, no moon, no ghosts. Just a drive through shadowy streets to the sound of fountains, and the very special echo of travertine pavements.

During the first week Blair helped me find and fit
out an apartment. It consisted of five rooms in an old
palace across the river and within stone's-throw of the
basilica of Santa Maria in Trastevere. The rooms
were high and damp and bad Eighteenth Century.
The ceiling of the salone was modestly coffered and
there were bits of crumbling stucco in the hall, still
tinted with faint blues and pinks and gilt; every
morning's sweeping carried off a bit more of some cu-
pid's curls or chips of scroll and garland. In the
kitchen there was a fresco of Jacob wrestling with the
angel, but the stove concealed it. We passed two days
in choosing chairs and tables, in loading them upon
carts and personally conducting them to our mean
street; in haggling over great lengths of gray-blue bro-
cade before a dozen shops, always with a view
toward variety in stains and unravellings and creases;
in selecting from among the brisk imitations of ancient candelabra those which most successfully simu-
lated age and pure line.

The acquisition of Ottima was Blair's triumph.
There was a trattoria at the corner, a lazy casual
talkative wine-shop, run by three sisters. Blair studied
them for a time, and finally proposed to the intelligent middle-aged humorous one that she come and
be my cook "for a few weeks." Italians have a horror
of making long-term contracts and it was this last
clause that won Ottima. We offered to take on any
man she recommended to help her with the heavier
work, but she clouded at that and replied that she
could very well do the heavier work too. The removal
to my rooms must have arrived as a providential solu-
tion to some problem in Ottima's life, for she attached
herself passionately to her work, to me, and to her
companions in the kitchen, Kurt the police dog and

8

Messalina the cat. We each winked at the others' failings and we created a home.

The day following our arrival, then, we called upon the latest dictator of Rome and found a rather boyish spinster with an interesting and ailing face, fretful bird-like motions and exhibiting a perpetual alternation of kindness and irritability. It was nearly six when we walked into her drawing-room in the Palazzo Barberini and found four ladies and a gentleman seated a little stiffly about a table conversing in French. Mme. Agaropoulos gave a cry of joy at seeing Blair, the absent-minded scholar to whom she was so attached; Miss Grier echoed it. A thin Mrs. Roy waited until something had been dropped into the conversation about our family connections before she could relax and smile. The Spanish Ambassador and his wife wondered how on earth America could get on without a system of titles whereby one might unerrably recognize one's own people, and the Marquesa shuddered slightly at the intrusion of two coarse young redskins and began composing mentally the faulty French sentence with which she would presently excuse herself. For a time the conversation blew fitfully about, touched with the formal charm of all conversation conducted in a language that is native to no one in the group.

Suddenly my attention was caught by a tension in the room. I sensed the tentatives of an intrigue without being able to gather the remotest notion of the objectives. Miss Grier was pretending to babble, but was in reality quite earnest, and Mrs. Roy was taking notes, mentally. The episode resolved itself into a typical, though not very complicated, example of the Roman social bargain, with its characteristic set of ramifications into religious, political and domestic life.

In the light of information received much later, I call your attention to what Mrs. Roy wanted Miss Grier to do for her; and what Miss Grier asked in return for her services:

Mrs. Roy had narrow eyes and a mouth that had just tasted quinine; while she spoke her ear-pendants rattled against her lean clavicles. She was a Roman Catholic, and in her political activity a Black of the Blacks. During her residence in Rome she had occupied herself with the task of bringing the needs of certain American charitable organizations to the attention of the Supreme Pontiff. Slander attributed a diversity of motives to her good works, the least damaging of which was the hope of being named a Countess of the Papal States. The fact is that Mrs. Roy was pressing audiences in the Vatican with the hope of inducing His Holiness to commit a miracle, namely to grant her a divorce under the Pauline Privilege. This consummation, not without precedent, depended upon a number of conditions. Before taking any such step the Vatican would ascertain very carefully how great the surprise would be in Roman Catholic circles; American cardinals would be asked in confidence for a report on the matron's character, and the faithful in Rome and Baltimore, without their being aware of it, would be consulted. This done it would be well to gauge the degree of cynicism or approval the measure would arouse in Protestants. Mrs. Roy's reputation happened to be above reproach, and her right to a divorce indisputable (her husband had offended under every category: he had been unfaithful; he had lapsed from a still greater faith; and he had become an *animæ periculum*, that is, he had tried to draw her into an irreverent argument over the liquefaction of the blood of St. Januarius); but the Protestant *imprimatur* was needed. Whose opinion would be more valuable for this purpose than that of the austere directress of the American Colony? Miss Grier would be approached—and both women knew it—through channels exquisite in their delicacy and resonance; and if an uncertain note were sounded from the Palazzo Barberini, the familiar verdict Inexpedient would be returned to the petitioner, and the question never reopened.

Mrs. Roy having so much to ask from Miss Grier, wanted to know if there were any service she could render in return.

There was.

No Italian work of art of the classic periods may leave the country without an enormous export tax. How then did Mantegna's "Madonna between St. George and St. Helen" ever arrive at the Alumnae Hall of Vassar College without passing through the customs? It was last seen three years before in the collection of the poor Principessa Gaeta: it was so ascribed in the reports of the Minister of Fine Arts for the following years, in spite of the rumor that it was being offered to the museums of Brooklyn, Cleveland and Detroit. It changed hands six times, but the dealers, savants and curators were so taken up with the problem as to whether or not St. Helen's left foot had been retouched by Bellini (as Vasari affirms) that it had never occurred to them to ask if it had been registered at the border. It was finally bought by a mad old Boston dowager in a lavender wig who, dying, bequeathed it (along with three spurious Botticellis) to that college with which her vicious spelling alone would have prevented her association in any capacity save that of trustee.

The Minister of Fine Arts at Rome had just heard

11

of the donation and was in despair. When the thing became known his position and reputation would be gone. All his vast labors for his country (*exempli gratia:* he had obstructed the disinterment of Herculaneum for twenty years; he had ruined the façades of twenty gorgeous Baroque churches in the hope of finding a Thirteenth-Century window; etc., etc.) would avail him nothing in the storms of Roman journalism. All loyal Italians suffer at the sight of their art treasures being carried off to America: they are only waiting for some pretext to rend an official and appease their injured honor. The Embassy was already in agonies of conciliation. Vassar could not be expected to give up the picture, nor to pay a smuggler's duty. Tomorrow morning the Roman editorials would picture a barbarous America stealing from Italy her very children and references would be made to Cato, Aeneas, Michelangelo, Cavour and St. Francis. The Senatus Romanus would sit on every bit of delicate business that America was endeavoring to recommend to Italian favor.

Now Miss Grier, too, was a trustee of Vassar. She had a flattering position in the long processions that formed in June among the sun-dials and educative shrubs. She was ready to pay the fine, but not until she had placated the city fathers. This could be done by obtaining the favorable votes of the committee that was to sit that very evening. This committee was composed of seven members, four of whose votes she already commanded; the other three were Blacks. For the matter to be dropped in the interest of the Princess Gaeta a unanimous verdict was necessary.

If Mrs. Roy descended at once to her car, she would have time to drive to the American College in the Piazza di Spagna and confer with dear omniscient

12

Father O'Leary. Marvellous are the acoustics of the Church! Before ten that evening the three Black votes would be decently cast for conciliation. It was Miss Grier's task over the tea-table to convey this long exposition to Mrs. Roy and to intimate the ineffable return she, Miss Grier, would be able to make for any favors. This was complicated by the necessity of making sure that neither Mme. Agaropoulos nor the Ambassadress (men don't matter) suspected the least collusion. Fortunately the Ambassadress could not understand rapid French, and Mme. Agaropoulos, being sentimental, could be continually distracted from the main issue by little sops of prettification and pathos.

Miss Grier played these several cards with the economy and precision of a faultless technique. She had that quality which is a peculiar part of the genius that invests great monarchs, and which we see notably in Elizabeth and Frederick, the power of adjusting threats to just the degree that stimulates, yet does not antagonize. Mrs. Roy understood at once what was expected of her. She had been packing committees and conciliating soured Papal chamberlains and Italian political *dévotés* these many years; trading in influence was her daily portion. Moreover joy can exert the happiest sort of influence on the intelligence and she felt her divorce was at hand. She rose hastily.

Will you excuse me if I run? she murmured. I told Julia Howard I would call for her at Rosali's. And I have an errand in the Piazza di Spagna.

She bowed to us and fled. What emotion is it that lends wings to such matter-of-fact feet and blitheness to such thin dispositions? The next year she married a young French yachtsman, half her age; she settled down in Florence and gave birth to a son. The Blacks

13

no longer talked votes when she entered their drawing-rooms. Vassar retains the painting and in its archives a letter from the Italian Secretary for Foreign Affairs which reads like a deed of gift. The influence of a work of art upon the casual passerby is too subtle for determination, but one has faith to believe that the hundreds of girls who pass beneath the Mantegna daily draw from it impulses that make them nobler wives and mothers. At least that is what the Ministry promised the College.

When the others had gone, Miss Grier made a face after them, lowered the lights and bade us talk about New York. She seemed to take some pleasure in such exotic company as ourselves, but her mind strayed until suddenly jumping up, she smoothed out the folds of her gown and bade us hurry off, dress, and come back to dinner at eight. We were surprised but equal to it, and dashed off into the rain.

At once I harried Blair for more facts about her. He could give me little; the portrait of her mind and even of her features lies in the following account of her ancestry that I made out for myself by reading between the lines and by studying the photographs of a history of the Griers, written by a second cousin, for considerations.

It seems that her great-grandfather had gone to New York in 1800, suffering from ill-health. He took an old house in the country and intended spending his days like a hermit, studying the prophetic passages of the Bible and encouraging the multiplication of four pigs that he had brought across the water in a basket. But his disposition improving with his affairs, he soon discovered himself to be married to the heiress of Dawes Corners, Miss Agatha Frehestocken, the death of whose parents, ten years later, united two farms of considerable extent. Their children, Benjamin and Anne, were brought up with such education as fell to them on rainy afternoons at the caprice of their father. Our Miss Grier's grandfather, a crafty single-minded country boy, disappeared for many years into a whirlpool of obscure activity in town, becoming in turn potboy, newspaper devil and restaurant manager. At last he revisited his parents and forced them to permit his using their land as security for some railroad investments. We have his picture at this stage: the daguerreotype of the Dutch yokel with the protruding lower lip and grinning pugnacious eyes is reproduced in any history of the great American fortunes. Probably the gentle art of horse-whipping one's parents was revived that Sunday evening at Dawes Corners for Anne intimates that she was directed to take her knitting into the feed-house and sit on sacks until she was recalled. The old father cursed the son roundly from the imprecatory psalms and had his curious revenge: the worm of religious introspection was stirred in the brain of Benjamin Grier and a strain of ill-health in his body. Success came of it: he became a deacon and a millionaire at about the same time; he was presently directing five railroads from a wheel-chair. His parents died in a Washington Square mansion, unforgiving to the end.

Benjamin married the daughter of another magnate, a girl who in another age and faith would have retired to a convent and eased the poverty of her mental and spiritual nature in a perpetual flow of damp unexplainable tears. She bore a sickly son to the world of brownstone, a son in whom the esthetic impulse, stifled during so many generations of Griers and Halletts, attained a piteous flowering, a passion for the operas of Rossini, and for things he fondly took to be Italian, garish rosaries, the costumes of the peasants of Capri, and the painting of Domenichino. He married a firm sharp woman, older than himself, who had deliberately chosen him in the vestry of the Presbyterian Church. They were incredibly wealthy, with that wealth that increases in the dark and, untended, doubles in a year. With the affiliation of this determined Grace Benham one last offspring was made possible to the Grier line,—our Miss Grier. To the score of governesses that trod sobbing on one another's heels, she appeared a monster of guile and virulence. She was dragged without rest from New York to Baden-Baden, from Vevey to Rome, and back again; and she grew up without forming any attachment to place or person. Her parents died when she was twenty-four and finally sheer solitude did what exhortation could not do: her character softened in an attempt at piteously luring people to talk to her, live with her, to fill somehow the moneyed emptiness of her days.

Such an account of her extraction, if she read it, would have neither interested her nor embarrassed her. Her mind lay under the hot breath of a great fretfulness; she lived to ridicule and insult the fools and innocents of her social circle. In this fretfulness floated all the enthusiasms and frustrations of her line: her great-grandfather's gloom, her grandfather's whip and his dread of the Valley of Bones, her grandmother's red eyes and her father's repressed loves for the Normas and Semiramides of the Academy of Music. She was restless too, with the masculine capacities inherited from her grandfather, the capacities of a business magnate, that given her sex and situation could find their only outlet in a passion for making

16

women tremble and a mania for interfering in the affairs of others. She was with all this a woman of intelligence and force; she ruled her eccentric and rebellious parish with acrid pleasure and at her death the drawing-rooms of Rome resounded with a strange wild murmur of muted joy.

Her portrait is not complete without an account of her strangest habit, due partly to the sleepless nights of a lifetime of illness, and partly to the fear of ghosts instilled in her by governesses when she was a girl. She was never able to sleep until the coming on of dawn. She feared to be alone; toward one in the morning she could be found urging her last callers to stay a little longer; *c' est l'heure du champagne*, she would say, offering them that untimely inducement. When finally they went away she would devote the rest of the night to music, for like the German princes of the Eighteenth Century she maintained her own troup of musicians.

These sessions before dawn were not vaguely and sentimentally musical; they were to the last degree eclectic. In one night she would hear all the sonatas of Scriabin or the marches of Medtner; in one night both volumes of the Well-Tempered Clavichord; all the Handel fugues for organ; six Beethoven trios. Gradually she won away from the more easily appreciated music altogether and cultivated only what was difficult and cerebral. She turned to music that was interesting historically and searched out the forgotten rivals of Bach and the operas of Grétry. She paid a group of singers from the Lateran choir to sing her endless Palestrina. She became prodigiously learned. Harold Bauer would listen meekly to her directions on phrasing Bach—he averred that she had the only truly contrapuntal ear of the age—and the Flonzaleys

17

acceded to her request to take certain pages of Loeffler a little faster.

In time I encountered a number of people who for one reason or another were unable to sleep between midnight and dawn, and when I myself tossed sleepless or when I returned late to my rooms through the deserted streets—at the hour when the parricide feels a cat purring against his feet in the darkness—I pictured to myself old Baldassare, in the Borgo, former Bishop of Shantung, Apostolic Visitor to the Far East, rising at two to study with streaming eyes the Church Fathers and the Councils, marvelling he said, at the continuous blooming of the rose-tree of Doctrine; or of Stasia, a Russian refugee who had lost the habit of sleeping after dark during her experience as nurse in the War, Stasia playing solitaire through the night and brooding over the jocose tortures to which her family had been subjected by the soldiers of Taganrog; and of Elizabeth Grier listening the length of her long shadowed room to some new work that d'Indy had sent her or bending over the score while her little troup revived the overture to *Les Indes Galantes*.

When we remounted the steps an hour later, then, we found the guests already arrived and awaiting their hostess. Among other privileges Miss Grier had long reserved to herself a prerogative of royalty, that of being the last arrival at one's own parties. In the hall the maître-d'hôtel gave me a note reading: Please take in Mlle. de Morfontaine, a high Merovingian maiden who may invite you to her villa at Tivoli. In a few moments Miss Grier had slipped in and was greeting her guests in a hurried zigzag across the room. She was dressed after a costume-plate by

18

Fortuny, conceived in salamander red and black. About her neck hung a rare medal of the Renaissance, much larger than any other woman would have ventured to wear.

As this woman wanted to be in a position to hear every word spoken at her table Rome had long had good reason to complain of the crowded arrangements of her dinners; we were packed together like the hurried diners at Modane. But she had still other conventions to challenge: she discussed the food; she reversed the direction of conversation from the right to the left hand at the least convenient opportunities; she talked to the servants, chattily; she shifted the conversation from French to English or Italian capriciously; she referred to guests who had been invited but had not been able to come. One suddenly became aware that she was not eating the courses that were served to us. She began with a little bowl of breadcrumbs and walnuts; to this she added later—while we confronted a *faisan Souvaroff* dressed with truffles and *foie gras* and graced with that ultimate dark richness which it is the privilege of Madeira to confer on game—an American cereal, soaked in hot water and touched with butter. Nor could she restrain herself from teasing her guests in a dangerous way, and with almost inspired precision: a political Duke on his dull speeches; Mrs. Osborne-Cady on the career as a concert-pianist that she had sacrificed to a more than usually disappointing home-life. For a moment at the beginning of the meal her electric eyes paused at my place and she began to murmur ominously, but thinking better of it she ordered the servant to offer me some more *oeufs cardinal* adding with a sort of insolence that they were the only *oeufs cardinal* that one could eat in Europe and that Mémé (the elder Prin-

19

cess Galitzine) was a little fool to vaunt her chef, who had received his training in railway-stations, etc., etc.

The high Merovingian maiden at my left was Mademoiselle Marie-Astrée-Luce de Morfontaine, daughter of Claude-Elzéar de Morfontaine and Christine Mézières-Bergh; her grandfather Comte Louis Mézières-Bergh had married Rachel Krantz, the daughter of the great financier Maxi Krantz, and had been the French ambassador to the Vatican in 1870. She was then, excessively rich, for she owned, they said, more shares in the Suez Canal than the Rothschilds: She was tall, large-limbed and bony, without somehow being too thin. Her high white face, framed between two carnelian ear pendants, recalled some symbolical figure in a frieze of Giotto, out of drawing, but radiating gaunt spiritual passions. She had a hoarse voice and a rapt manner, and for the first ten minutes said many foolish things because her mind was afar off; one felt vaguely that it would come around in its own time. This it presently did and with considerable impact. She outlined to me the whole Royalist movement in France. She seemed to believe as passionately in its aim as she depised its practice. There can be no king in France, she cried, until catholicism has had a great revival there. France cannot be great save through Rome. We are Latins; we are not Goths. They are forcing alien systems upon us. Eventually we shall find ourselves, our kings, our faith, our Latin hearts. I shall see France return to Rome before I die, she added clasping her hands before her chin. I replied faintly that both the French and Italian temperaments seemed to me singularly unrepublican, whereupon she laid her long pale hand upon my sleeve and invited me to come that week-end to her villa.

You will hear the whole argument, she said. And the Cardinal will be there.

I asked which Cardinal? The pain on her face showed me that at least for the circle in which she moved there were not seventy cardinals, but one.

Cardinal Vaini, of course. The College at present is singularly free of uninteresting priests, but surely the only cardinal with learning, with distinction, with charm, is Cardinal Vaini.

I had so often encountered learning, distinction and charm (to say nothing of piety) in the lower reaches of the Church that I was shocked to learn that these qualities were so rare higher up.

Besides she added, what other is friendly to France, the rebellious daughter? You have not yet met the Cardinal? Such knowledge! And to think that he will not write! If I may say it without disrespect His Eminence is afflicted with a sort of—inertia. The whole world is waiting for an explanation of certain contradictions in the Fathers; he is the only man who can do it; yet he remains silent. We beg him with prayers. It is in his power to effect the reentry of the Church into literature. Perhaps he might single-handed carry through the cause we all have so at heart.

I asked shyly what cause this might be.

She turned toward me with some surprise. Why, the promulgation of the Divine Right of Kings as a dogma of the Church. We hope to have an Ecumenical Council called for that purpose within the next twenty-five years. I thought that of course you knew; in fact I assumed that you were one of our workers.

I replied that I was both an American and a Protestant, an answer that I felt relieved me of the burden of being a catholic royalist.

Oh, she said, we have many adherents who at first glance would appear to have no interest in the movement: we have Jews and agnostics, artists, and, yes, even anarchists.

I now felt quite sure that I was sitting beside an insane person. They don't lock you up when you have millions, I said to myself. The idea of trying to collect a Council, in the Twentieth Century, to give crowns a supernatural sanction and to enroll the sanction among the articles of obligatory belief, was no mere pious revery; it was lunacy. We were prevented from returning to the subject that evening, but several times I found her spacious half-mad glance resting on me with greater implication of intimacy than I was quite ready to acknowledge.

I will send the car for you at eleven, she murmured as she passed me in leaving the table. You must come. I shall have a great favor to ask of you.

On returning to the drawing-rooms I found myself beside Ada Benoni, daughter of a popular senator. Although she seemed almost too young to go out in the evening, she had that soft cautious sophistication of well-brought-up Italian girls. I asked her almost at once if she would tell me about the Cabala.

Oh, the Cabala's only some people's joke, she answered. There is no Cabala, really. But I know what you mean. And the young girl's eyes carefully estimated the distance between us and the company on all sides. By Cabala they mean a group of people that are always together and have a lot in common.

Are they all rich? I asked.

No ... she answered thoughtfully. We mustn't

speak so loudly. Cardinal Vaini can't be rich, nor the Duchess d'Aquilanera.

But they're all intellectual?

The Princess d'Espoli isn't intellectual.

Then what have they in common?

Oh, they haven't anything in common, except ... except that they despise most people, you and me and my father and so on. They've each got one thing, some great gift, and that binds them together.

Do you believe that they work together and plan trouble here and there?

The girl's forehead wrinkled and she reddened slightly. No, I don't think they mean to, she said softly.

But they *do*? I insisted.

Well, they sit over there in Tivoli and talk about us and somehow, without knowing it, they then *do* something.

How many of them do you know?

Oh, I know all of them a little, she replied quickly. Everybody knows all of them. Except, of course, the Cardinal. I love them all too. They're only bad when they're together, she explained.

Mlle. de Morfontaine has asked me to spend the week-end at her villa in Tivoli. Will I see them there?

Oh, yes. We call that the hotbed.

Is it all right? Have you any advice to give me before I go?

No.

Yes, you have.

Well, she admitted, drawing her eyebrows together, I advise you to be ... to be stupid. It's hard. You must expect them to be very cordial at first. They have a way of getting very excited about people and

23

then getting tired of them and dropping them. Except every now and then they find someone they like and they adopt him or her for good, and there's a new member of the Cabala. Rome's full of people who went through the rapids and didn't stick. Miss Grier's especially that way. She's just met you lately, hasn't she?

Why, yes,—just this afternoon.

Well, she'll have you around every minute of the day for a while. She's coming over in a minute to ask you to stay to her midnight supper. She has famous midnight suppers.

But I can't. I was here to tea and immediately asked to dinner. It would be ridiculous to stay to midnight. . . .

It's not ridiculous in Rome. You're just getting into the rapids, that's all. Everybody cultivates their friendships in rushes. It's very exciting. Don't try and fight against it. If you do that you lose the best of everything. Do you want to know how I know about your being in the rapids? Well, I'll tell you. My fiancé was to have come to the dinner tonight, and an hour before, a note was brought to his house asking him to come next Friday instead and go to the Opera also. She does that often and it only means that she has found some new friend she insists on keeping by her that evening. Of course the second invitation, the consoling one, is always bigger and more showy than the first, but we get angry.

I should say so. I'm sorry I was the one to prevent . . .

Oh, that's all right, she answered. Vittorio's out waiting for me in the car now.

So it was that when Blair and I presented ourselves before Miss Grier to take our leave, she drew me aside with an irresistible vehemence and standing against my ear said: You are to come back here tonight. There will be some people in to a late supper whom I want you to meet. You can, can't you?

I made some show of protest, and the effect was appalling. But, my dear young man, she cried, I'll have to ask you to trust me. There is something of the first importance that I want to put to you. The fact is I have already telephoned a very dear friend of mine. . . . Please now, just as a favor to me, put off what you had planned. There's a very great service we want to ask you.

Of course with that I fairly folded up, as much with surprise as compliance. Apparently the whole Cabala wanted me to do favors.

Thank you, thank you so much. About twelve.

It was then about ten. Two hours to kill. We were about to go to the Circus, when Blair exclaimed:

Say, do you mind if I drop in and see a friend of mine for a minute. If I'm going Tuesday I ought to say goodbye and see how he is. Do you hate sick people?

No.

He's a nice fellow, but he hasn't long to live. He's published some verse in England; one of the thousand, you know. It got an awful rap. Maybe he's quite a poet, but he can't get over that diction. He's awfully adjectival.

We climbed down the Spanish Steps and turned in at the left. On the stairs Blair stopped and whispered: I forgot to tell you that he's watched over by a friend, a sort of water-colourist. They're dead-poor and it's all they can do to get a doctor. I meant to lend them some more money—what have you with you?

We assembled a hundred lire and knocked at the door. Receiving no answer we pushed it open. There was a lamp burning in the further of two mean rooms. It stood beside a bed and cast its light on the remorseless details of a barricade built during the last stages of consumption against a light vaulter; bowls and bottles and stained cloths. The sleeping invalid was sitting high in bed, his head turned away from us.

The artist must have gone out for a minute to look for some money, said Blair. Let's stay around a bit.

We went into the other room and sat in the dark looking at the moonlight that filled the Fountain of the Boat. There were fireworks on the Pincian Hill in memory of some battle on the Piave and the tender green of the sky seemed to tremble behind the Chinese blooms that climbed the night. A friendly tram entered the square at intervals, stopped inquiringly, and bustled out again. I tried to remember whether Virgil had died in Rome ... no, buried near Naples. Tasso? Some piercing-sweet pages of Goethe, the particular triumph of Moissi who brings to them his wide-open eyes and elegiac voice. Presently we heard a call from the next room: Francis. Francis.

Blair went in: I guess he's gone out a minute. Can I do something for you? I'm going in a day or two and I called around to see how much better you are. Would it tire you if we sat with you a bit? ... Come on in, say!

For the moment Blair had forgotten the poet's name and our introduction was slurred over. The sick man looked his extremity, but his fever gave to his eyes an eager and excited air; he seemed willing to listen or to talk for hours. My eye fell upon a rough pencilled note that lay on the table beyond the invalid's reach: Dear Dr. Clarke: he spat up about two cupfuls of blood at 2 P.M. He complained so of hunger that I had to give him more than you said. Be back at once. F.S.

Have you been able to write anything lately? Blair began.

No.

Do you read much?

Francis reads to me. He pointed to a Jeremy Taylor on his feet. You're Americans, aren't you? I have a brother in America. In New Jersey. I was to have gone over there.

The conversation lapsed, but he kept staring at us, smiling and bright-eyed, as though it were swift and rare.

By the way, are there any books you'd like us to lend you?

Thank you. That would be fine.

What, for instance?

Anything.

Think of one you'd like especially.

Oh, anything. I'm not particular. Only I suppose it would be hard to find any translations from the Greek?

Here I offered to bring in a Homer in the original and stammer out an improvised translation.

Oh, I should like that most of all, he cried. I know Chapman's well.

I replied, unthinking, that Chapman's was scarcely Homer at all, and suddenly beheld a look of pain, as of a mortal wound, appear upon his face. To regain control of himself he bit his finger and tried to smile. I hastened to add that in its way it was very beauti-

27

ful, but I could not recall my cruelty; his heart seemed to have commenced bleeding within him.

Blair asked him if he had almost enough poems for a new book.

I don't think about books any more, he said. I just write to please myself.

But the insult to Chapman had been working in him; he now turned his face away and great tears fell upon his hands. Excuse me. Excuse me, he said. I'm not well, and I seem to ... to do this about nothing.

There was a search for a handkerchief, but none being found he was persuaded to use mine.

I don't want to go away without seeing Francis, said Blair. Do you know where I might find him?

Yes, yes. He's around the corner at the Café Greco. I begged him to go and get some coffee he'd been here all day.

So Blair left me with the poet, who seemed to have forgiven me and was ready for the hazards of further conversation. Feeling it was better I did the talking, I began to discourse upon everything, on the fireworks, on the wildflowers of Lake Albano, on Pizzetti's sonata, on a theft in the Vatican library. His face showed clearly what matter pleased him; I experimented on it, and discovered that he was hungry for hearing things praised. He was beyond feeling indignant at abuses, beyond humor, beyond sentiment, beyond interest in any bits of antiquarian lore. Apparently for weeks together in the wretched atmosphere of the sick-room Francis had neglected to speak highly of anything and the poet wanted before he left the strange world to hear some portion of it praised. Oh, I laid it on. His eyes glowed and his hands trembled. Most of all he desired the praise of poetry. I launched upon a history of poetry, calling

28

the singers by name, getting them wrong, assigning them to the wrong ages and languages, characterizing them with the worn epithets of an encyclopedist, and drawing upon what anecdotage I could,—all bad, but somehow marshalling the glorious throng. I spoke of Sappho; of how a line of Euripides drove mad the citizens of Abdera; of Terence pleading with audiences to come to him rather than to the tight-rope walkers; of Villon writing his mother's prayers before the great picture-book of a cathedral wall; of Milton in his old age, holding a few olives in his hand to remind himself of his golden year in Italy.

Quite suddenly in the middle of the catalogue he burst out fiercely: I was meant to be among those names. I was.

The boast must have revolted me a little and my face have shown it, for he cried again: I was. I was. But now it's too late. I want every copy of my books destroyed. Let every word die, die. When I'm dead I don't want a soul to remember me.

I murmured something about his getting well.

I know more about it than the doctor, he replied, staring at me with stern fury. I studied to be a doctor. And I watched my mother and brother die, just as I am dying now.

There was no answer for that. We sat silent. Then in a gentler voice he said:

Will you promise me something? My things weren't good enough; they were just beginning to be better. When I am dead I want you to make sure that Francis does what he promised. There must be no name on my grave. Just write: Here lies one whose name was writ in water.

There was a noise in the next room. Blair had returned with the water-colourist. We withdrew. The poet was too sick to see us again and when I came back from the country he had died and his fame had begun to spread over the whole world.

BOOK TWO

————

# MARCANTONIO

La Duchessa d'Aquilanera was a Colonna and came
from the conservative wing of a family that cannot
forget its cardinalitial, royal and papal traditions. Her
husband had come of a Tuscan house that had received its illustration by the Thirteenth Century, was
praised in the histories of Machiavelli and execrated
in Dante. Neither family had counted a misalliance in
twenty-two generations, and even in the twenty-third
incurred only such stigma as attaches to marriage
with an illegitimate Medici or a Pope's "niece." The
Duchess could never forget—among a thousand similar honors—that her grandfather's grandfather, Timo-
leo Nerone Colonna, Prince of Velletri, had carried
many an insulting message to the ancestors of the
present King of Italy, the old but apologetic house of
Savoy; and that her father had refused a Grandeeship
at the court of Spain because it had been withheld
from his father; and that through herself she carried

31

to her son the titles of Chamberlain of the Court of Naples (if there were one), Prince of the Holy Roman Empire (if that superb organization had only survived) and Duke of Brabant, a title which unfortunately reappears among the pretensions of the royal families of Spain, Belgium and France. She had the best of claims to an Altesse, and even to an Altesse Royale; at least to the Sérénissime, for her mother had been the last member of the royal family of Craburg-Hottenlingen. She had the largest cousinage outside the Buddhist priesthood. The heralds of the European courts bowed to her with a particular distinction, realizing that by some accident many diverse and lofty lines converged in her odd person.

She was fifty when I met her, a short, black-faced woman with two aristocratic wens on the left slope of her nose, yellow, dirty hands, covered with paste emeralds (an allusion to her Portuguese claims; she was Archduchess of Brazil, if Brazil had only remained Portuguese), lame with the limp that pursues the Della Quercia, just as her aunt had been epileptic with the epilepsy of the true Vani. She lived in a tiny apartment in the Palazzo Aquilanera, Piazza Araceli, from the windows of which she watched the sumptuous weddings of her rivals, ceremonies to which she had been invited, but dared not attend, foreseeing that she would be assigned to places that fell below her pretensions; to accept a humble seat would be to admit that one had relinquished the whole bundle of vast historic claims. She had left many a great function abruptly on discovering that her chair was behind some of those Colonna cousins who had cast away all right to aristocratic distinction by marrying theatre women or Americans. She refused to be seated behind pillars among dubious Neapolitan titles

32

—in the shadow of her own family tombs; to be left among the footmen at the door of a musicale; to be invited at the eleventh hour; and to be kept waiting in antechambers. For the most part she clung to her ugly stuffy rooms, brooding on the disregarded glories of her line and envying the splendors of her richer relatives. The fact is that from the point of view of a middle-class Italian she was not really poor; but she was too poor to afford the limousine and livery and great entertainments; to be without these and yet invested with her pretensions was to be poorer than the last nameless body fished out of the Tiber.

Recently however she had begun to receive unexpected and thrilling recognitions. Little though she went out, when she did appear in society, her austere face, her majestic limp, and her strange jewels carried conviction. People were afraid of her. The arbiters of precedence in Rome dared at last to intimate to the Odescalchi and Colonna and Sermoneta that this almost shabby little woman whom they snubbed and shoved like some half-wit poor relation, had every right to precede them at a formal function. French circles, such as had not lost all seigneurial deferences under the sponge of republicanism, recognized her ultramontane alliances. She was the first to notice the improvement in her reception, and if a bit bewildered it did not take her long to set her sails to the unexpected breeze. She had a son and daughter to advance and it was for them that she now resolved to immolate her pride. From the earliest signs of her rehabilitation she forced herself to sally out into the world, and finding that her stock was higher in the international colony she stopped distastefully to call upon the American peeresses and on the South American representatives. Eventually she found herself at

33

Miss Grier's midnight suppers. The reflection of the consideration she received in such places finally reached her own people and she was gradually spared the more obvious humiliations.

It became necessary for her now to drop her former friends, the dull soured old women, more plaintive than herself, and with less reason, with whom she had been accustomed to fret away the long afternoons and evenings behind the drawn blinds of the Piazza Araceli. She was obliged likewise to abandon a sordid habit that linked her no less surely to the previous centuries, namely that of rushing into law-suits. The innate capacity for affairs which abounded in this woman had found during the days of her obscurity this extraordinary outlet. She went about scenting out old claims and deeds, the slips of tradesmen and the subtle omissions of lawyers. She was always protecting her shyer friends from imposition, and she was always successful and often made a good deal of money. She employed obscure boy-lawyers and when she was called upon as a witness, relying on her distinctions to prevent her being interrupted, she used the occasion as an opportunity to sum up the whole case. The middle classes seeing in the morning paper that S. A. Leda Matilda Colonna duchessa d'Aquilanera was attacking the City of Rome over the valuation of property near a railroad, or contesting the bill of some popular stationer or fruiterer on the Corso, suffered willingly the inconvenience of holding a seat in court for hours in order to see the malignant resourceful woman and to hear her trenchant sarcasms and her irresistible accumulation of evidence. Yet her relatives had always sneered at this passion, failing to see that she represented more

34

clearly than themselves the qualities that had always gone to characterize the aristocracy.

It was this woman then whom we confronted when we returned at midnight for our third engagement that day in the old palace. Supper was served in a larger, brighter apartment than I had yet seen. As I entered the huge doorway my eyes fell upon a strange figure that I knew at once must be a Cabalist. A short, dark, ugly woman, holding a cane between her knees was staring at me with magnificent fierce eyes. With the bodiced dress and eagle's head I became aware of her jewels, seven hugh lumpy amethysts strung about her neck on a golden rope. I was presented to this witch who at once, and by the blackest art, made one like her. On hearing that Blair was leaving Rome shortly she centered her attention on me.

For a moment she sat before me, sliding the end of her stick nervously about on the floor, drawing in her upper lip, and gazing hard into my eyes. She asked me my age. I was twenty-five.

I am the Duchess d'Aquilanera, she began. What language shall we speak? I think we will talk English. I do not talk it good, but we must be plain. It must be so you must understand me quite perfectly. I am a great friend of Miss Grier. I have often talked over with her a great problem—a sorrow, my young friend—that is in my home. Suddenly tonight at seven o'clock she call me up on the telephone and told me she have found someone who could help me: she mean you. Now listen: I have a son of sixteen. He is important because he is somebody. How you say?—he is a personage. We are of a very old house. Our family has been in the front of Italy, everyone in her

35

triumph and in her trouble. You are not sympathetic to that kind of greatness in America, not? But you must have read history, no? ancient times and the middle time and like that? You must realize how important the great families are ... have always been to ... countries ...

(Here she grew nervous, and blew several bubbles and expended herself in those splendid Italian gestures denoting difficulty, perhaps futility, and resignation before the impossible. I hastened to assure her that I had great respect for the aristocratic principle.)

Perhaps you have and perhaps you haven't, she said at last. In all events, think of my son as a prince whose blood contains all sorts of kings and noble people. Well, now I must tell you he has fallen in bad ways. Some women have got hold of him and I do not know him any more. All our boys in Italy go that way when they are sixteen, but Marcantonio, my God, I do not know what is the matter with him and I shall go crazy. Now in America you are all descended from your Puritans, are you not, and your ideas are very different. There is only one thing to do, and that is: you must save my boy. You must talk to him. You must play tennis with him. I have talked to him; the priest has talked to him, and a good friend of mine, a Cardinal, has talked to him and still he does nothing but go to that dreadful place. Elizabeth Grier says that most boys in America at your age are just ... naturally ... good. You are *vieilles filles;* you are as temperate as I do not know what. It's very strange, if it's true, and I do not think I believe it; at all events it's not wise. At all events you must talk to Marcantonio and make him stay away from that dreadful place or we shall go mad. My plan is this: next Wednesday we are going for a week to our beautiful

36

villa in the country. It is the most beautiful villa in Italy. You must come with us. Marcantonio will begin to admire you, you can play tennis and shoot and swim and then you can have long talks and you can save him. Now, won't you do that for me, because no one has ever come to you in such trouble as I have come to you in today?

Hereupon, in sudden fear that all her efforts had been in vain, she began waving her stick to attract Miss Grier's attention. That lady had been watching us from a corner of her eye and now came running up. The Duchess burst into a flood of tears, crying into her pocket handkerchief: Elisabetta, speak to him. Oh, my God, I have failed. He not want us and all is lost.

I was divided between anger and laughter and kept muttering into Miss Grier's ear: I'd be glad to meet him, Miss Grier, but I can't lecture the fellow. I'd feel like a fool. Besides what would I do with a whole week. . . .

She's put it to you wrongly, said Miss Grier. Let's not say anything more about it tonight.

At this the Black Queen began rolling about in her chair, the motions preparatory to rising. She rammed her stick against my shoe for leverage on the polished floor and stood up. We must pray to God to find another way. I am a fool. I do not blame the young man. He cannot realize the importance of our family.

Nonsense, Leda, said Miss Grier, firmly in Italian. Be quiet a moment. Then turning to me: Would you like to pass a week-end at the Villa Colonna-Stiavelli, or not? There's no stipulation about lecturing the Prince. If you like him, you'll feel like talking to him anyway, and if you don't like him, you're welcome to leave him alone.

Two Cabalists were begging me to take a glimpse

of the most famous of Renaissance villas, one moreover that was obstinately closed to the public and that had to be peered at from the road half a mile away. I turned to the Duchess and bowing low accepted her invitation. Whereupon she kissed the shoulder of my coat, murmured with a beautiful smile: Christiano! Christiano! and bidding us goodnight, passed bowing from the room.

I shall see you Sunday at Tivoli, said Miss Grier, and tell you all about it there.

During the next few days my mind lay under the dread of the two engagements that lay ahead of me: the week-end at the Villa Horace and the missionary enterprise at the Villa Colonna. I stayed in my rooms, depressed, reading a little, or took long walks through the Trasteverine underworld, thinking about Connecticut.

The car that called for me Saturday morning already contained a fellow-guest. He introduced himself as M. Léry Bogard, adding that Mlle. de Morfontaine had offered to send for us separately, but that he had taken the liberty of requesting that we be called for together, not only because any company in crossing the Campagna is better than none, but because he had heard many things of me that led him to believe that we would not be uncongenial. I replied in that language wherein all courtesy sounds sincere, that the possibility of being congenial to so distinguished a member of the French Academy and to so profound a scholar was a greater honor than I dared hope for. These overtures did not tend to chill the encounter. M. Bogard was a fragile elderly gentleman, immaculately dressed. His face was delicately tinted by exquisite reading and expensive food,

38

russet and violet about the eyes, his cheeks a pale plum from which rose the ivory-white of his nose and chin. His manner was soft and conciliatory, expressed for the most part in the play of his eyelids and hands, both of which fluttered in unison like petals about to fall upon the breeze. I spoke hesitantly of the pleasure I had derived from his works, especially from those pages, so faintly tinctured with venom, on Church History. But now he cried out at once: Do not mention them! My early indiscretions! Horrible! What would I not give to withdraw them. Can that nonsense have reached as far as America? You must let your friends know, young man, that those books no longer represent my attitude. Since then I have become an obedient son of the Church and nothing would give me greater comfort than to hear that they had been burned.

What may I tell my friends now represents your real views? I asked.

Why read me at all? he cried in mock grief. There are too many books in the world already. Let us read no more, my son. Let us seek out some congenial friends. Let us sit about a table (well-spread, pardi!) and talk of our church and our king and perhaps of Virgil.

My face must have shown a trace of the suffocation I experienced at this plan of life, for M. Bogard became at once more impersonal. The country we are traversing now, he said, has known stirring times ... and he began an instructive travelogue, as though I were some stupid acquaintance, his hostess' son, and as though he were not, nor ever had been, a distinguished scholar.

On arriving at the Villa we were met by the steward and shown to our rooms. The Villa had been a monastery for many years and in purchasing it Mlle. de Morfontaine had obtained likewise the adjoining church which still served the peasants of the hillside. She claimed that the Villa was the very one that Maecenas had given to Horace: local tradition affirmed it; the foundations were of the best opus reticulatum; and the location fulfilled the rather vague requirements of classical allusion; even onomatopoeia testified, declared our hostess, asserting that from her window the waterfall could be literally heard to lisp

" . . . domus Albuniae resonantis
Et praeceps Anio ac Tiburni locus et uda
Mobilibus pomaria rivis."

In furnishing her monastery our hostess had combined, as best she could, a delight in esthetic effects and a longing for severity. A long low rambling plaster building, without grace of line, was the Villa Horace. Disordered rose gardens surrounded it, with intentionally neglected gravel paths, and chipped marble benches. One entered a long hall at the end of which several steps descended to a library. The hall was lined with doors at regular intervals on both sides, doors to what had once been cells now thrown together into reception rooms. Many of these doors stood open during the day and the long corridor, paved with russet tile, was striped with the sunshine that fell across it. The ceiling had been coffered, and like the doors touched with dark green and gilt, and with that rich wasted brick-red that is the color of Neapolitan tiles. The walls were yellow white, of caked and crumbling plaster, and the beauty of the view with the optical illusion of distance and the depth and the lightness of the library seen like some great green-golden well at the further end, appealed to that sense of balance and one's tactile imagination

40

as do the vistas in the paintings of Raphael whose spell is said to reside in that secret. To the left lay the reception rooms, carpeted in one color, hung with tabernacles and Italian primitives, while huge candelabra, pots of flowers and tables covered with brocades and crystals and uncut jewels, relieved the severity of unfreshened walls. Towards the end of the hall at the right one ascended a few steps to the refectory, the barest room in the house. By day the refectory was a meaningless casual clubroom. Luncheon was a negligible affair at the Villa; one's conversation must be saved for dinner; at luncheon one barely looked at one another, one talked about the last rains and the next drought, or any subject that did not faintly allude to the devouring passions of the house, religion and aristocracy and literature. The beauty of the refectory was purely a matter of lighting and at eight o'clock the greatness of the room lay in the pool of wine-yellow light that was shed on the red table cloth, the dark green crested plates, the silver and the gold, the wineglasses, the gowns and decorations of the guests, the ambassadorial ribbons, the pontifical violets, and the little army of satin-clad footmen that suddenly appeared from nowhere.

On the night of my arrival the Cardinal was the last to appear at dinner, and entered directly into the refectory where we stood waiting for him. His expression was benignant, even beaming. While he blessed the meal, Mlle. de Morfontaine knelt on her admirable yellow gown and M. Bogard dropped on one knee and shaded his eyes. The grace was in English, a strange affair discovered by our erudite guest among the literary remains of some disappointed Cambridge parson.

41

Oh, pelican of eternity,
That piercest thy heart for our food,
We are thy fledglings that cannot know thy woe.
Bless this shadowy and visionary food of substance,
Whose last eater shall be worm,
And feed us rather with the vital food of
Dreams and grace.


The Cardinal, though unimpaired in mind and
body, looked all of his eighty years. The expression of
dry serenity that never left his yellow face with its
drooping moustache and pointed beard gave him the
appearance of a Chinese sage that has lived a century. He was born of peasants on the plain between
Milan and Como, and had begun his education at the
hands of the local priests who soon discovered in him
a veritable genius for latinity. He was passed upward
from school to school gaining in his progress all the
prizes the Jesuits had to offer. The attention of a
large body of influential churchmen was gradually
drawn to him and at the time of his graduation from
the great college on the Piazza Santa Maria sopra
Minerva (presenting a thesis of unparalleled brilliance and futility on the forty-two cases in which
suicide is permissible and the twelve occasions on
which a priest may take up arms without danger of
homicide) a choice between three great careers was
offered to him. The details of each had been prepared
under the highest patronage: he might become a
fashionable preacher; or one of the courtier-secre-
taries of the Vatican; or a learned teacher and dispu-
tant. To the amazement and grief of his professors he
suddenly announced his intention of following a road
that to them meant ruin; he declared for Missions.
His foster-fathers raged and wept and called on

heaven to witness his ingratitude; but the boy would hear of nothing less than the Church's most dangerous post in Western China. Thither in due time he departed with scarcely a blessing from his teachers who had already turned their attention to more docile if less brilliant pupils. Through fire, famine, riots, and even torture, the young priest labored for twenty-five years in the province of Sze-chuen. This missionary fever however did not entirely spring from piety. The boy, conscious of the great powers raging within him, had been throughout his youth insolent, contemptuous of his teachers and of his companions. He knew and despised every type of a churchman to be found in Italy; never had he seen a thing adequately done by them, and now he dreamed of a field of work where he would be answerable to no fool. In the whole realm of the Church there was only one region that filled his requirements; a month's travelling by crude wagon separates one from the next priest in Sze-chuen. There, then, after a shipwreck, some months of slavery, and other experiences that he never related, but which reached the world from his native helpers, he settled in an inn, dressed as a native, grew a pigtail, and lived among the villagers for six years without mentioning his faith. He passed the time studying the language, the classics, the manners, ingratiating himself with the officials and so perfectly identifying himself with the daily life of the city that in time he all but lost the odor of foreignness. When at last he began to declare his mission to those merchants and officials in whose homes he had become an almost nightly visitor his work was rapid. Perhaps the greatest of all the Church's missionaries since the Middle Age, he turned many a compromise that was destined to shock Rome profoundly. He somehow

43

achieved a harmonization of Christianity and the religions and accepted ideas of China that had its parallel only in those daring readings that Paul discovered in his Palestinian cult. So subtle were the priest's adaptations that it never occurred to his first converts to be even conscious of repudiating their old faith until at last after twenty lectures he showed them how far they had gone and how charred were the bridges that lay behind them. Once he had them baptized however, he could give them only the bitterest bread to eat: the foundations of his cathedral lay squarely on a score of martyrs' graves, but once built suffered no further assault and grew slowly and irresistibly. Finally sheer statistics did what envy could not prevent and he was made a bishop. At the end of his fifteenth year in the East he returned to Rome for the first time and was received with cold dislike. His health had been partly undermined, and he was granted a year's repose, during which he worked in the Vatican library on a thesis relative to nothing in China, the donation of Constantine. This was considered shocking in a missionary and when it was published its learning and impersonality won it the neglect of the ecclesiastical reviewers. He was treated with condescension by the courtiers of the Palace; by implication they described to him their idea of his great creation in Western China: a low mud-brick meeting-house and a congregation of beggars who pretended to a conversion in order to be fed. He did not trouble to describe to them the stone cathedral with two awkward but lofty towers, the vast porch, the schools and library and hospital; the processions on Feast days carrying garish but ardent banners entering the great cavern of the Church and singing the correctest Gregorian; nor of the governmental honors,

44

the tax-exemptions, the military respect during revolutions, the co-operation of the city.

At last he returned, willingly enough, to sink himself for another ten years into the remote interior. His visit to Rome had not altered his boyish attitude toward his fellowmen. He had heard strange tales about himself,—how he had amassed a huge fortune by taking bribes from the Chinese merchants, how he had interpreted the atonement in Buddhist terms and had allowed pagan symbols to be stamped upon the Host itself.

The ecclesiastical honors that eventually arrived must have been extravagantly deserved, for they came without his or any friend's negotiation. Sheer accomplishment must so have stared the Vatican in the face that it had felt torn from its hands the trophies it was accustomed to relinquish only on the receipt of petitions bearing ten thousand signatures or at the instance of wealth or power. To receive these new distinctions, the Bishop returned to Rome again after an absence of ten years. This time he meant to remain in Italy, having decided that henceforth his work would be better in the hands of natives. The ecclesiastics viewed this return with considerable trepidation, for if he returned as a scholar eager for doctrinal debates they dreaded seeing exposed their lack of interest or equipment: if he came as a critic of the Propaganda, they were all in danger. They watched him settle down with two Chinese servants and an absurd peasant woman whom he insisted on referring to as his sister, in a tiny villa on the Janiculum, join the Papal Archaeological Society and apply himself to reading and gardening. Within five years his retirement had become a greater embarrassment to the Church than his pamphlets might have been. His

45

fame among Romanists outside Rome was unbounded; every distinguished visitor rushed from the station to get an introduction to the recluse of Janiculum; the Pope himself was a little tried by the zeal of visitors who imagined that His Holiness enjoyed nothing better than discussing the labors, the illness, and the modesty of the Cathedral Builder of China. English Catholics and American Catholics and Belgian Catholics who did not understand the exquisite subtlety of these matters and should let them alone, kept crying: Why isn't something being done for him? He humbly refused a high honorary Librarianship in the Vatican, but his refusal was not accepted and his name crowned the stationery; the same thing happened with the great committees on Propaganda; he did not appear at the meetings, but no speech was so influential as the report of chance words let fall in conversation with disciples at the Villino Wei Ho. His very lack of ambition frightened the Churchmen; they supposed it must arise from a similar emotion to that which kept Achilles sulking in his tent, and dreaded the moment when he would ultimately arise, swinging his mighty prestige and crush them for the honors they begrudged him; finally he was offered the Hat, by a committee from the College all in a perspiration lest he refuse it. This time he accepted their offer and went through the forms with a rigid decorum and with an observance of traditional minutiae that had to be elaborately explained to his Irish American colleagues.

It would be hard to say what his thoughts were those clear mornings as he sat among his flowers and rabbits, a volume of Montaigne fallen on to the gravel path from the tabouret beside him, what were his thoughts as he gazed at his yellow hands and listened to the hushed excitement of the Aqua Paola exclaiming in eternal praise of Rome. He must surely have asked himself often in what year his faith and joy had fled. Some said that he had become attached to a convert who had relapsed into paganism; some said that one day under torture he had renounced Christianity to save his life from the hands of brigands. Perhaps it was only that he had attempted the hardest task in the world and found it not so difficult after all; and reflecting that he could have built up a huge fortune in the financial world with half the energy and one-tenth the gifts; that he was the only person living who could write a Latin that would have entranced the Augustans; that he was the last man who would be able to hold in his head at one moment all the learning of the Church; and that to become a Prince of the Church required nothing but a devoted indifference to its workings,—reflecting on these things he may well have felt the world not to be worth the thunder of admiration and applause that was so continually mounting to Heaven in its praise. Perhaps one of the other stars is more worthy of one's best effort.

Grace concluded, the meal could not be begun until the Cardinal was informed as to Alix. But where's Alix?

Alix is always late.

Are you sure she's coming?

She telephoned this afternoon, that ...

Now isn't that too bad of her! She's coming in panting when the dinner's half over. Then apologies. Father, you're too kind to her. You always forgive her directly. You must act cross.

We must all act cross.

Everybody look angry when Alix comes in.

I had assumed that the conversation of the Cabala *in camera* would be vertiginous. If I anticipated the wit and eloquence of its table-talk I dreaded their gradual discovery that I was tongue-tied or doltish. When, therefore, the conversation at last broke forth I had the mixed sensation of discovering that it was not unlike that of a house party on the Hudson. Wait, I told myself, they will warm up. Or perhaps it is my presence here that prevents them from being at their best. I recalled the literary tradition that the gods of antiquity had not died but still drifted about the earth shorn of the greater part of their glory—Jupiter and Venus and Mercury straying through the streets of Vienna as itinerant musicians, or roaming the South of France as harvesters. Casual acquaintances would not be able to sense their supernaturalism; the gods would take good care to dim their genius but once the outsider had gone would lay aside their cumbersome humanity and relax in the reflections of their ancient godhead. I told myself that I was the obstacle, that these Olympians chattered and chaffed for a season until my departure, when the air would change,—what divine conversation. . . .

Presently in burst their Alix, the Princess d'Espoli, panting and a-flutter with apologies. She knelt to the Cardinal's sapphire. No one looked the least bit cross. The very servants beamed. We are to know a great deal about the Princess later; suffice it to say that she was a Frenchwoman of the utmost smallness and elegance, sandy-haired, pretty, and endowed with a genius for conversation in which every shade of wit, humor, pathos and even tragic power followed in close succession. Within a few moments she was enchanting the company with a lot of nonsense about a horse who had started talking on the Pincian Hill and the

48

efforts of the Police Force to suppress such an aberration of nature. As I was presented to her she murmured quickly: Miss Grier told me to tell you that she will be here at about ten-thirty.

After dinner Mme. Bernstein played the piano for a time. She was still the power behind the great German banking house. Without ever venturing into her sons' offices or directors' meetings she yet disposed of all the larger decisions of the firm by curt remarks at their dinner tables, by postscripts to her letters and by throaty injunctions at the moment of saying goodnight. She wanted the sensation of having retired from its direction; her whole middle life had been expended in a magnificent display of generalship and financial imagination, yet she could not keep her mind off its problems. The friendship of the Cabala was beginning to reconcile her to advancing age, and drawing her further and further into her love for music.

As a girl she had often heard Liszt and Tausig in her mother's home; by dint of never playing Schumann or Brahms she had kept her fingers all silver and crystal, and even now, practically in her old age, she evoked the great era of virtuosi, a time when the orchestra had not led piano technique into a desperate imitation of brass and strings. Mlle. de Morfontaine sat holding in the cup of her hand the muzzle of one or other of her splendid dogs. Her eyes were filled with tears, but whether they were the facile tears of her half-mad nature or the witness of memories brought back on the tide of Chopin's sonata, we cannot know. The Cardinal had retired early and the Princess sat in the shadows, not listening to the music, but pursuing some of the phantoms of her most secretive mind.

Barely had the army with banners ceased drilling in the wintry sunlight of the last movement when a servant whispered to me that the Cardinal wished to see me.

I found him in the first of the two small rooms that had been set aside for him at the Villa. He was writing a letter, standing up to it at one of those high desks known to the clerks of Dickens and the illuminators of the Middle Age. I was later to receive many of those famous letters, never more nor less than four pages long, never falling short of their amazing suavity, never very witty nor vivid yet never untouched from beginning to end by the quality of their composer's mind. Whether he declined an invitation or suggested a reading of Freud's book on Leonardo, or gave suggestions on the feeding of rabbits, always from the first sentence he foresaw his last and always like a movement from Mozart's chamber-music the whole unit lay under one spirit and the perfection of details played handmaid to the perfection of the form. He seated me in a chair that suffered all the light that was in the room, treating himself to a fine shadow.

He began by saying that he had heard that I was to keep an eye on Donna Leda's son for a while.

I became warm and unintelligible in an effort at protesting that I could guarantee nothing; that I was most reluctant; and that I still reserved the right to withdraw at any moment.

Let me tell you about him, he began. Perhaps I should say first that I am a sort of old uncle in the family, and their confessor for many years. Well,—this Marcantonio. What shall I say? Have you seen him?

No.

The boy is full of good things. He ... he ... Full of

50

good things. Perhaps that's his trouble. You say you haven't met him yet?

No.

Everything seemed to start well. He was good in his studies. He made a lot of friends. He was particularly good in the ceremonial that his rank requires, his attendance at Court and at the Vatican. His mother was a little anxious about his boyish dissipations. She had his father in mind, I suspect, and wanted the boy to get over them as soon as possible. Donna Leda is a more than usually foolish woman. She was very pleased when he set up his own apartment off on the Via Po and became very secretive about it.

Here the Cardinal began to grope about again, perhaps surprised at his own awkwardness. Presently however he gathered up the reins with new determination and said: And then, my dear young man, something went wrong. We thought he would go through the usual experience of a Roman young man of his class and come out. But he has never come out. Perhaps you can tell me why this young fellow couldn't have had his five or six little affairs and gotten over it?

I showed myself as quite unequal to answering this question. In fact I was so amazed at the five or six little liaisons for a boy of sixteen, that it was all I could do to keep my face casual. I wanted badly not to appear shocked and endeavored by a lift of an eyebrow to imply that the boy might have a score if he liked.

Marcantonio, continued the priest, went around with a group of boys older than himself. His greatest wish was to be like them. You could see them at the races, in the music-halls, at Court, in the tea-rooms and hotel lobbies. They wore monocles and American hats, and all they talked about was women and their own successes. Euh ... perhaps I should begin at the beginning.

There was a pause.

He was first initiated—perhaps I should use a stronger word—on Lake Como. He used to play tennis with some very warm little South American girls, heiresses from Brazil, I believe, from whom no secrets were hid. I fancy our Tonino merely meant to pay them a shy compliment or two, a sudden kiss under the laurel-bushes. But he soon found himself with a little ... a sort of Rubens riot on his hands. Well, it began in imitation of his older friends. From imitation it went to an exercise of vanity. What was Vanity became Pleasure. Pleasure became a Habit Habit became a Mania. And that's where he is now.

There was another pause.

You must have heard of how certain insane persons become enormously intelligent—that is, they become sly and secretive—trying to conceal their delusion from their guards? Yes; and I am told that vicious children perform feats of duplicity worthy of the most expert criminals, in an effort to conceal their tricks from their parents. You have heard of such things? Well, that is where Marcantonio is now. What can be done? Some people would say that we should let him go and make himself thoroughly sick. Perhaps they are right, but we should like to step in before that, if possible. Especially since there has come a new development into the story.

My mood at that moment was overwhelmingly against new developments. In the distance I could hear that Mme. Bernstein had resumed her Chopin. I would have given a lot for the power of being rude enough to leap for the doorknob and bid my host goodnight, a long goodnight to the wallowing little Prince and his mother.

Yes, continued the Cardinal, his mother has at last found a marriage for him. To be sure she does not believe there is a house in the world that can bring any new distinction to her own, but she has found a girl with an old name and some money and expects me to do the rest. But the girl's brothers know Marcantonio. They are in the group I described to you. They refuse to permit the marriage until Marcantonio has, well— been quiet for a while.

Now my face must have shown a rich mixture of horror and amusement and anger and astonishment, for the Cardinal became perplexed. You never can tell what will surprise an American, he probably said to himself.

No, no. Excuse me, Father. I can't, I can't.

What do you mean?

You want me to go to the country to hold him down to a few weeks of temperance. I don't understand how you can mean such a thing, but you do. He's a sort of Strassburg goose whom you want to stuff with virtue, don't you, against his marriage. Don't you see . . . ?

You exaggerate!

Excuse me if I sound rude, Father: No wonder you couldn't make an impression on the boy,—you didn't believe in what you were saying. You don't really believe in temperance.

Believe in it. Of course I do. Am I not a priest?

Then why not make the boy . . . ?

But after all, *we are in the world.*

I laughed. I shouted with a laughter that would have been insulting, if it hadn't contained a touch of hysteria. Oh, I thank thee, dear Father Vaini, I said to myself. I thank thee for that word. How clear it makes all Italy, all Europe. *Never try to do anything against the bent of human nature.* I came from a colony guided by exactly the opposite principle.

Excuse me, Father, I said at last. I can't go on with it. Under any conditions I should feel an awful hypocrite talking to the boy. But if I knew it were only a measure to keep him good a month or two I should feel ten times more so. It can't be argued; it's just a matter one feels. I must tell Miss Grier I cannot visit her friend. She is driving out here at ten-thirty. If you will excuse me I shall go and find her in the music-room now.

Do not be angry with me, my son. Perhaps you are right. Probably I do not believe these things.

Hardly had I re-entered the music-room with my revolt written all over me when the Princess d'Espoli came forward. By that telepathy which the Cabala employed in its affairs she already knew that I had to be persuaded all over again. She made me sit down beside her and with the briefest outlay of those gifts of suppliance and enchantment of which she held the secret, she won my promise. In two minutes she had made it seem the most natural thing in the world that I should play stern older brother to a gifted drifting friend of hers.

As by the click of some invisible stage-manager Miss Grier entered.

How are you, how are you? she said, trailing her russet draperies across the tiles toward me. You can't guess who drove me out. I must hurry back. The Lateran choir is coming to sing Palestrina to me about twelve,—perhaps you know the motets from

54

the Song of Songs? No? Marcantonio brought me here. He loves high-powered cars, and as his mother can't give him one I let him play with mine. Can you come out and meet him now? You'd better get your coat. Do you like night rides?

She led me out to the road where behind two blinding headlights a motor was humming impatiently. Antonino, she called. This is an American friend of your mother's. Do show him the car for half an hour, will you? Don't kill anybody.

An incredibly slight and definite little elegant, looking exactly his sixteen years, with spark-like black eyes bowed stiffly to me in the faint light over the wheel. Italian princes do not rise at the approach of ladies.

Don't hurt my car or my friend, Marcantonio.

No.

Where are you going?

But he did not choose to answer and the aroused motor drowned out the lady's questions. For ten minutes we sat in silence while the road rose to the headlights. After a harrowing struggle with his own selfishness Don Marcantonio asked me if I wanted to take the wheel. Assured that nothing would alarm me more, he settled down to driving with an almost voluptuous application. He made nice distinctions with grades and corners, took long descents cantabile-mente, and played scherzi on cobblestones. The outlines of the Alban hills stood out against the stars that like a swarm of golden bees recalled that haughty Barberini who had declared that the sky itself was the scutcheon of his house. All lights were out on the farms, but occasionally we passed through a village whose francobollo shop showed a lantern and a group of card players. Many a wakeful soul in those enormous family beds must have turned over, crossing himself, at the sighing whistle of our flight.

Presently however the driver wanted to talk. He asked a great many questions about the United States. Could one plunge into the life of the Wild West any minute? Were there many big cities as big as Rome? What language was spoken in San Francisco? in Philadelphia? Where did our athletes train for the Olympic Games? Was the public allowed to watch them? Did I know about such things? I replied that at school and college one couldn't help picking up hints on form and training. He then disclosed the fact that at the Villa Colonna he had directed the gardeners to make a running-track, cinders and hurdles and pit and shed and embanked corners. And that we were to use it every morning. He dreamed of himself doing incredible distances in incredible time. He outlined a plan to me whereby under my direction he would begin by running a mile every morning, and should add a half-mile daily for weeks. This would go on for years and then he would be ready to enter the Paris Olympics of 1924.

In my head the nerves of astonishment had been a little fatigued lately, what with Mlle. de Morfontaine and her Ecumenical Council, the Cardinal and his tolerances, Miss Grier and her cereals. But I confess they received no small twinge when this frail and emptied spirit announced his candidacy for the world's record in long runs. Not without sly intention I began to outline the sacrifices that such an ambition would entail. I touched on diet and early hours and early rising; he accepted them eagerly. I then skirted those self-denials that would touch him more particularly, and now with a mounting exaltation, with an almost religious fire, he pledged himself to all temperance. The fact that I was astonished shows my immaturity. I thought I was witness to a great conversion. I told myself that he wanted to be saved; that he was rolling up outside forces that might protect himself from his weakness; and that he hoped to find in athletics a deliverance from despair.

Returning to the Villa we found the company still listening to music. As we entered the room all eyes were turned towards us and I knew that for the present the Cabala had laid aside all activity and was brooding over one thing, the rescue of Donna Leda's son.

On arriving at my rooms in Rome I found several notes from a Mr. Perkins of Detroit, a successful manufacturer who had crossed with me. Mr. Perkins, descending upon Italy for the first time, was resolved to see it at its best. There were no collections so private but that he was able to secure letters of admittance; no savants too occupied but that he obtained their services as ciceroni; audiences he obtained with the Pope were, as he called them, "super-special"; excavations not yet open to the public suffered his disappointed peerings. Some secretary at the Embassy must have mentioned that I had already made some Italian acquaintances, for there were these notes from him reminding me that he wanted to know some real Italians. He wanted to see what they were like in their homes, and he expected me to show him some. Mind, real Italians. I wrote him at once that all the Italians I knew were half French or half American, but assured him that when I had actually isolated a native I would bring them together. I added that I was leaving for the country, but would return in a week or two and see what could be done.

To the country then I went, being driven for the greater part of a day by Marcantonio himself. His enthusiasm for running had by no means abated; in fact it seemed to have gone from strength to strength, probably because of some lapses from strict training in the interval. It was late afternoon and a red sunset was filtering through a blue dusk when we entered the great gates of the park. There was first a forest of oaks; then a mile of open lawn with some hurrying sheep: then a pineta with a brook; the farmhouses in a cloud of doves; the upper terrace with a perspective of fountains; and at last the casino with the Black Queen trailing her garments of dusty serge across the driveway of powdered shell. There was little time to admire the orange-brown front of the villa roughened with wreaths and garlands that were crumbling away before the sun and rain, or the famous frieze of the women in Ariosto's poems, recalling the days when Pope Sylvester Lefthand held here his academy and invented the Sylvestrian sonnet-form. All I could do was to conceal my pleasure at the discovery that I was to live by candle-light in rooms that though the originals of hundreds of bad copies on Long Island, were here the secret shame of their owners. My hosts' ideal of residence was a hotel on the Embankment and they all but breathed an apology for the enormous rooms to which I was conducted, and in which I stood transfixed, lost in antiquarian dreams until Marcantonio knocked on the door to call me to supper.

At table I was presented to Donna Julia, Marcantonio's half-sister, and to a spinster cousin of the family, always present, always silent and whose lips never ceased moving, as solitaries' must, to the measure of her inner thoughts. Like all girls of her class Donna Julia had never been alone for more than a half-hour in all her life. Her immense talents for being bad had been balked at every turn; they had been forced to take refuge in her eyes. She had never even been allowed to read anything more inflammatory than the comedies of Goldoni and I Promessi Sposi, but she guessed at a criminal world and presently when marriage suddenly opened up to her every freedom she played her part in it. Donna Julia was a little stiff, almost ugly with her level baleful regard. She kept silent most of the time, was utterly incurious of me, and seemed chiefly occupied in angling for her brother's evasive glance so as to plant into it a triumphant significant idea.

One retired early at the Villa Colonna. But Marcantonio, for whom my simplest remarks were astonishing, would stop in at my room and talk for hours over some glasses of Marsala. No doubt his mother, noting the visits through her half-opened door down the hall, assumed with great satisfaction that I was reading lectures on hygiene. But, especially as the week advanced, we were chiefly taken up with a diagram that showed day by day how the little champion had run and in what time.

It must have been at the end of a week of this that in one of our late conversations his friendliness suddenly turned into contempt. A week's preoccupation with unsentimental matters now took its revenge. Back into his mind flooded the images of passion, and he wanted to boast. Perhaps he saw that prowess on the field was not to be his, and his egoism being athirst for all possible superlatives, he must replace it with a catalogue of the first prizes he had won in another arena. He recalled the Brazilian girls under the arbors of Como. He described how he had returned to Rome after that initiation bent on seeing whether the game was as easy as it had seemed. Suddenly his eyes had been opened to a world he had not dreamed of. So it was true that men and women were never really engaged in what they appeared to be doing, but lived in a world of secret invitations, signals and escapes! Now he understood the raised eyebrows of waitresses and the brush of the usher's hand as she unlocks the loge. It is not an accident that the wind draws the great lady's scarf across your face as you emerge from the door of the hotel. Your mother's friends happen to be passing in the corridor outside the drawing-room, but not by chance. Now he discovered that all women were devils, but foolish ones, and that he had entered into the true and only satisfactory activity in living—the pursuit of them. One minute he was exclaiming at the easiness of it; the next he described its difficulties and subtlety. Now he sang the uniformity of their weakness and now the endless variety of their temperaments. Next he boasted of his utter indifference and his superiority to them; he knew their tears but he did not believe they really suffered. He doubted whether they had souls.

To incidents that were true he added others that he wished had been true. To his acquaintance with a corner of Rome he added a fourteen-year-old's vision of a civilization where no one thought about anything but caresses. This fantasy took him about two hours. I listened without a word. It must have been this that undermined his exhilaration. He had been talking to impress me. Impressed I certainly was; no New Englander could help it; but I knew that a great deal depended on my not showing it. Perhaps it was his sudden realization that, seen through my eyes, these adventures were not enviable; perhaps it was that the black tide of reaction licked close on the heels of such pride; perhaps it was just truth finding room for utterance in his mounting fatigue,—at all events, there was strength left for one more outburst: I hate them all! I hate it. There's no end to it all. What shall I do? And he fell on his knees beside the bed and buried his face in the side of the mattress, his hands feverishly pulling at the cover.

Priests and doctors must often hear the cry Save me! Save me! I was destined to hear it from two other souls before my Roman year was over. Who now thinks it uncommon?

I scarcely know what I said when my turn at last came around. All I know is that my mind whipped up to its subject with a glee. Heaven only knows what New England divines lent me their remorseless counsels. I became possessed with the wine of the Puritans and alternating the vocabulary of the Pentateuch with that of psychiatry I showed him where his mind was already slipping: I pointed out wherein he already resembled his uncle Marcantonio, no mean warning; I made him see that even his interest in athletics was a symptom of his disintegration; how that he was incapable of fixing his mind on the general interests of man, and how everything he thought and did—humor, sports, ambition—presented themselves to him as symbols of lust.

My little tirade was effective beyond all expectation and for a number of reasons. In the first place, it had the energy and sincerity which the Puritan can always draw upon to censure those activities he cannot permit himself,—not a Latin demonstration of gesture and tears, but a cold hate that staggers the Mediterranean soul. Again, all my words had already their dim counterpart in the boy's soul. It is the libertine and not the preacher who conceives most truly of the ideal purity and soundness, because he pays it out, coin by coin, regretfully, knowingly, unpreventably. All my words went to rejoin their prototypes in Marcantonio's mind. Again, how could I know that he had arrived but recently at that stage of failure when one's whole being reverberates, as with some bell of despair, with the words: I shall never get out of this. I am lost. Again, I found out later that Marcantonio had a streak of religious frenzy in him, that for a year he had watched himself alternating communion and dissipation, the exaltation of the former itself betraying him into the latter and the despair of the latter driving him in anguish to the former. At last in sheer cynicism, after watching himself fail so often, he had missed Mass for several months. All these reasons go toward explaining the prostrating effect my brief and vindictive speech had. He cowered against the carpet, begging me to stop, gasping out his promises of reform. But having brought him to a conviction he might never attain again, I thought it unwise to let go. I had reserves of indignation left. But now he knelt crying on the carpet, covering his ears with his hands and shaking his wet face at me with all its terror and suppliance. I stopped and we stared at one another, darkly, trembling under our several headaches. Then he went to bed.

The next morning he seemed etherialized, made almost transparent by his new resolutions. He walked lightly and with an air of humility. No reference was made to the scene of the evening before, but his glances over the tennis net implied an obedience and a deference that were more annoying than impudence. After two sets we wandered over to the lower fountain and here stretched out on the semi-circular bench he slept for three hours. It seemed to me as I watched morning advance to noon and the sun penetrate his thin body in the delicious fatigues that follow hysterical outbursts, it seemed that it would not be rash to wonder if possibly we may have succeeded. I day-dreamed. From the formal terrace below the casino came the click of topiary shears; from the field where the ancient altar had been placed, drum-shaped and bearing an almost effaced frieze, came the shouts of some divinity students (to whom a little villa on the estate had been offered as a vacation house) playing football, their cassocks tucked up about their knees; from the pine wood the exclamations of two shepherds who sat whittling while their flock drifted almost imperceptibly to the road beyond. The fountain before me gave forth its varied sounds: the whir of its initial jet and the tinkle as it fell back into the first bowl; the drumtaps as this overflowed and slipped into the second; and the loud loquacity with which the lowest basin received all that came to it from every level. Tacitus lay unread upon my knee while my eyes followed the lizards that flashed in and out of the brilliant sunshine on the gravel, noting their confusion when a sudden breeze bent the poised veil of the fountain and swept us all with a fine mist. The monotony of light and the noise of water, of insects, and of doves in the farmhouses behind me, combined to recall those tremulous webs of sound that modern composers set shimmering above their orchestra, to draw across it presently on the oboes their bleating melody in thirds.

While I sat there a note was brought me from the house. Mr. Perkins of Detroit had heard I was at the Villa and from the hotel in the nearby town announced his intention of calling on me—lucky in having a pretext for entering the most inaccessible villa in Italy. I scribbled on the back of his envelope that an unfortunate event in the family prevented my asking him to the house at present.

The hot sunlight of the morning had gathered its storm and all afternoon we sat indoors. Marcantonio and Donna Julia attempted teaching me the Neapolitan dialect, while the silent cousin sat by, deeply shocked. But my lesson soon descended into a subtle and barbed quarrel between the teachers. It was conducted for the most part in rapid and hate-laden parentheses, far above my head, in their thick *argot*. What she taunted him about I can only guess. He was invariably beaten; he grew loud and angry. Twice he leaped around the table to strike her; she waited for the blow, stretching herself sleekly and looking up at him from her magnetic eyes. At length he urged me to come away from her and to go upstairs, and the two parted much as children of seven would with a bout of grimaces and a competition to have the last ugly word.

After dinner the war was resumed. The Duchess was nodding by the fire; the cousin was mumbling opposite her. And the two children sat in the shadows exchanging invective. I was made strangely uneasy by their curious quarreling. I excused myself and

64

went to bed. The last thing I saw was an infuriated blow that Marcantonio directed at his sister's shoulder and the last sound I heard was the tremolo of her provocative laughter as they tussled on the carved wooden chest in the corner. I debated with myself on the stairs: surely I had imagined it; my poor sick head was so full of the erotic narratives of the week; surely I imagined the character of mixed love and hate in those blows that were savage caresses, and that laughter that was half sneer and half invitation.

But I had not imagined it.

At about three I was awakened by Marcantonio. He was still dressed. He poured at my drowsy head a torrent of whirling words in which I distinguished nothing but a feverish reiteration of the phrase: You were right. Then he left the room as abruptly as he had come.

What luck Mr. Perkins had always had! Even now when he brought to bear all his American determination and broke into the gardens of the forbidden Villa, what guardian angel arranged that he should see the Villa at its most characteristic? Surely a rich old Italian villa is at its most characteristic when a dead prince lies among the rosebushes. When Frederick Perkins of Detroit leapt the wall in the crystal airs of seven in the morning, he discovered at his feet the body of Marcantonio d'Aquilanera, 14th prince and 14th duke of Aquilanera and Stoli, 12th duke of Stoli-Roccellina, marquis of Bugnaccio, of Tei, etc., baron of Spenestra, of Gran-Spenestra, seigneur of the Sciestrian Lakes; patron of the bailly of the order of San Stephano; likewise prince of Altdorf-Hottenlingen-Craburg, intendant elector of Altdorf-H-C; prince of the Holy Roman Empire, etc., etc.; chamberlain of the court of Naples; lieutenant and cousin of the Papal Familia; order of the Crane (f. class); three hours cold, and with a damp revolver clutched in his right hand.

# BOOK THREE

---

# ALIX

The Cabalists received the news of Marcantonio's death philosophically. The account of it which the bereaved mother gave to Miss Grier was a miracle of misunderstanding. According to her I had done wonders; in fact it was the suddenness and thoroughness of the boy's reformation that had broken his health. She, *she*, was to blame. She should have foreseen that continence was not to be expected of a mere lad; he had gone insane from an excess of virtue and shot himself from too much sanctity. These things are out of our hands, dear Leda, murmured Miss Grier. The Cardinal made no comment.

The Cabala went back to its usual occupations. Being the biographer of the individuals and not the historian of the group I shall not take up much space here with details of the discomfiture of Mrs. Pole (she had been impudent to Miss Grier), nor of the Renan performance (*L'Abbesse de Jouarre* was effectively not given as a benefit at the Constanzi). From a purely disinterested love of Church tradition they blocked the canonization of several tiresome nonentities that had been proposed to gratify the faithful in Sicily and Mexico. They saved the taxpayers of Rome the purchase of hundreds of modern Italian paintings, and the establishment of a permanent museum for them. They interested public opinion in the faint smell of drains that is wafted through the Sistine Chapel. When an oak forest fell ill in the Borghese Gardens no one but the Cabala had the sense to send to Berlin for a doctor. To tell the truth their achievements were not very considerable. I soon saw that I had arrived on the scene in the middle of the decline of their power. At first they thought they could do something about the strikes, and about the Fascismo, and the blasphemies in the Senate; and it was only after a great deal of money had been spent and hundreds of persons ineffectually goaded that they realized that the century had let loose influences they could not stem, and contented themselves with less pretentious assignments.

I came to see more and more of them. My youth and foreignness never ceased to amuse them and they were made almost uncomfortable by the knowledge that I so liked them. They thought they had outgrown being susceptible to being liked. From time to time they would point their fingers to where I sat staring at them in sheer wonder.

He's like an eager dog with his tongue out of his mouth, Alix d'Espoli would cry. What does he see in us?

He never loses hope that we will suddenly say something memorable, said the Cardinal looking at me musingly,—the look of a great talker who knows that for lack of a Boswell his greatness must die with him.

He comes from the rich new country that will grow more and more splendid while our countries decline to ruins and rubbish heaps, said Donna Leda. That's why his eyes shine so.

Why, no, cried Alix. I believe he loves us. Just simply loves us in a disinterested new world way. Once I had a most beautiful setter, named Samuele. Samuele spent all his life sitting around on the pavement watching us with a look of most intense excitement.

Did he bite? asked Donna Leda who had a literal mind.

You didn't have to give Samuele a sandwich to win his devotion. He liked to like. You won't be angry with me if every now and then I call you Samuele to remind me of him?

You mustn't talk about him in front of him, muttered Mme. Bernstein who was playing solitaire. Young man, get me my furs from the piano until these people remember themselves.

The Princess explained me. What fairer service can one render another? How could I do other than attach myself to one with so quick and gracious an interpretation.

The Princess was not really modern. As scientists gazing at certain almost extinct birds off Australia are able to evoke a whole lost era, so in the person of this marvellous princess we felt ourselves permitted to glimpse into the Seventeenth Century and to reconstruct for ourselves what the aristocratic system must have been like in its flower.

The Princess d'Espoli was exceedingly pretty in a fragile Parisian way; her vivacious head, surmounted by a mass of sandy reddish hair, was forever tilted

69

above one or other of her thin pointed shoulders; her whole character lay in her sad laughing eyes and small red mouth. Her father came of the Provençal nobility and she had spent her girlhood partly in provincial convent schools and partly climbing like a goat the mountains that surrounded her father's castle. At eighteen she and her sister had been called in from the cliffs, dressed up stiffly and hawked like merchandise through the drawing-rooms of their more influential relatives in Paris, Florence, and Rome. Her sister had fallen to an automobile manufacturer and was making the good and bad weather of Lyons; Alix had married the morose Prince d'Espoli who had immediately sunk into a profounder misanthropy. He remained at home sunk in the last dissipations. His wife's friends never saw or referred to him; occasionally we became aware of him, we thought, in her late arrivals, hurried departures and harassed air. She had lost two children in infancy. She had no life, save in other people's homes. Yet the sum of her sufferings had been the production of the sweetest strain of gaiety that we shall ever see, a pure well of heartbroken frivolity. Wonderful though she was in all the scenes of social life, she certainly was at her finest at table, where she had graces and glances that the most gifted actresses would fall short of conceiving for their Millamonts, and Rosalinds and Célimènes; nowhere has been seen such charm, such manners, and such wit. She would prattle about her pets, describe a leave-taking seen by chance in a railway station, or denounce the Roman fire departments with a perfection of rendering of Yvette Guilbert, a purer perfection in that it did not suggest the theatre. She possessed the subtlest mimicry, and could sustain an endless monologue, but the charm of her gift resided in the fact that it required the collaboration of the whole company; it required the exclamations, contradictions, and even the concerted shouts as of a Shakespearean mob, before the Princess could display her finest art. She employed an unusually pure speech, a gift that went deeper than a mere aptitude for acquiring grammatical correctness in the four principal languages of Europe; its source lay in the type of her mind. Her thought proceeded complicatedly, but not without order, in long looping parentheses, a fine network of relative clauses, invariably terminating in some graceful turn by way of climax, some sudden generalization or summary surprise. I once accused her of speaking in paragraphs and she confessed that the nuns to whom she had gone to school in Provence had required of her every day an oral essay built on a formula derived principally from Madame de Sévigné and terminating in a *concetto*.

Such rare personalities are not able to derive nourishment from ordinary food. Rumors of the Princess's strange stormy loves reached us continually. It seems that she was doomed to search throughout the corridors of Rome a succession of attachments as brief and fantastic as they were passionate and unsatisfied. Nature had decided to torment this woman by causing her to fall in love (that succession of febrile interviews, searches, feints at indifference, nightlong solitary monologues, ridiculous visions of remote happiness) with the very type of youth that could not be attracted by her, with cool impersonal learned or athletic young Northerners, a secretary at the British Embassy or Russian violinist or German archaeologist. As though these trials were not sufficient, society had added to them this aggravation, that her Roman hostesses, conscious of this failing and wishing to make sure that at their tables the Princess would display her finest flights, would intentionally include among their guests the Princess's latest infatuation to whom throughout the evening she would sing, like a swan, her song of defeated love.

As a mere girl, if I may presume to reconstruct the growth of her personality, she sensed the fact that there was in her something that a little prevented her making friends, namely, intelligence. The few intelligent people who truly wish to be liked soon learn, among the disappointments of the heart, to conceal their brilliance. They gradually convert their keen perceptions into more practical channels,—into a whole technique of implied flattery of others, into felicities of speech, into the euphemisms of demonstrative affection, into softening for others the crude lines of their dullness. All the Princess's perfection was an almost unconscious attempt at making friends of those who would first be her admirers, yet realizing that if she were too artistic they would be dazzled but repelled, and that if she were less than perfect they would dismiss her as a trivial bright hysteric. For many years she had practiced this babbling speech on her friends, unconsciously noting on their faces which tones of the voice, which appropriate fleck of the hands, which delayed adjectives were more and which less successful. In other words she had achieved mastery of a fine art, the all but forgotten art of conversation, under the impetus of love. Like some panic-stricken white mouse in the trap of a psychologist's experiment she had been seeking her ends by the primitive rules of trial and error, only to learn that at the last one is too bruised by the mistakes to enjoy the successes. The exquisite and fragile mechanism of her temperament had not been able to stand the strain laid upon it, the double exhaustion of inspiration and woe; and the lovely being was already slightly mad. She grew daily more light-headed and could be caught from time to time in moods that were variously foolish and pathetic. But her deepest wound was still to come.

James Blair and his notebooks were staying over in Rome after all. He had come upon some new veins of research. For him ten lifetimes would be all too short to pursue the horizons of one's curiosity. Think, he would say, it would take about ten years to work up the full critical apparatus to attack the historical problems surrounding the life of St. Francis of Assisi. It would take almost as many to get up the Roman road-system, the salt roads and the wheat roads,— God, the whole problem as to how the Rome of the Republic was fed. Another day he would be dreaming about starting on the eight or ten books in French and German on Christina of Sweden and her life in Rome; then one studied up Swedish and read the diaries and the barrels-full of notes; when one knew more about her than did anyone alive one passed on to her father and buried oneself for months in libraries to master the policies and the military genius of Gustavus Adolphus. Thus life stretched . . . bindings . . . bindings . . . catalogues . . . footnotes. One studied the saints and never thought about religion. One knew everything about Michelangelo yet never felt deeply a single work. James spent weeks of fascinated attention on the women of the Caesars and yet could scarcely be dragged to dinner at the Palazzo Barberini. He found all moderns trivial, and was the dupe of the historians' grand style which fails to convey the actuality (for Blair, the triviality) of their heros. The present casts a veil of cheapness over

73

the world: to look into any face, however beautiful, is to see pores and the folds about the eye. Only those faces not present are beautiful.

The fact is that quite early James Blair had been frightened by life (in a way which the Princess, in a moment of misery and inspiration, was to divine later with the cry: What kind of a stupid mother could he have had?) and had forever after bent upon books the floodtides of his energy. At times his scholarship resembled panic; he acted as though he feared that raising his eyes from the page he would view the world, or his share in the world, dissolving in ruin. His endless pursuit of facts (which had no fruit in published work and brought no intrinsic esthetic pleasure) was not so much the will to do something as it was the will to escape something else. One man's release lies in dreams, another's in facts.

All this resulted in a real unworldliness, which with his youth and learning and faintly *distrait* courtesy especially endeared him to older women. Both Miss Grier and Mme. Agaropoulos hovered about him with mothering delight and sighed with vexation at his obstinate refusal to come and see them. He reminded me of the lions that stare, unwinking and unseeing, at the crowd about their cage, the crowd that grimaces and waves admiring parasols, though the beast disdains to pick up even a biscuit from such vulgar givers.

At the time that the Princess's story begins he was engaged in establishing the exact location of the ancient cities of Italy. He was reading mediaeval descriptions of the Campagna and tracing through place-names, through dried water-courses, through cracked old paintings the exact position of disused roads and abandoned towns. He was learning about the country's former plants and animals: he was quite happy. Sometimes he made notes of all this, but for the most part he preferred to learn the truth and then forget it.

When it began to get cold in his room he serenely made use of mine, covering my tables with his vellum-bound folios, standing his pictures against my wall, and strewing my floors with his maps. He had dazzled one of the librarians at the Collegio Romano with his allusions and had obtained the privilege of bringing the material home.

One day the Princess d'Espoli came to see me. Ottima admitted her. She came in upon James Blair who was kneeling on the floor crawling from city to city on some yellow crested maps. His coat was off; his hair was in a tangle, and his hands were gray with dust. He had never met her and did not like her clothes. He did not want to be drawn into a conversation and stood, handsome and sulky, his glances stealing to the maps on the floor. Explained that I was out. Might not be back before. Would not forget to tell that.

Alix didn't mind. She even asked for some tea.

Ottima had just come in to begin thinking about dinner. While tea was making Alix asked to have the maps explained to her. Now the Princess was more capable of entering into an enthusiasm for old cities than most of the several hundred women of her acquaintance; but short of a doctorate in archaeology one does not enter upon such ground with James Blair. Coldly, haughtily, and with long quotations from Livy and Virgil, he harangued my guest. He dragged her remorselessly up and down the seven hills; he wrung her in and out of all the shifting beds of the Tiber. When I finally returned I found her sitting gazing at him over the edge of her tea-cup with a faintly mocking expression. She had not known that such a man was possible. Throughout the whole episode Blair had acted like nothing so much as a spoiled boy of seven interrupted in a game about Indians. It would be hard to say what had most captivated the Princess, but it was probably that trace of sturdy spoiled egotism. It might have been, in part, the cold douche of being unwelcome,—she who was the delight of the most delightful people in Europe, who had never entered a door without arousing a whirlpool of welcome, who had never come too early nor left too late,—suddenly she had tasted the luxury of being resented.

As soon as I arrived Blair took a swift and awkward departure.

But he's charming! He's charming! she cried. Who is he?

I told her briefly of his home, his progress through the universities, and his habits of study.

But he's extraordinary. Tell me: is he—shy, is he *boudeur* with everybody? Now perhaps I did something to annoy him? What could I have said, Samuele?

I hastened to reassure her. He's that way with everyone. And most people like him all the more for it. Especially older women. For example, Miss Grier and Mme. Agaropoulos adore him and all he does is to sit on their chairs inventing excuses for not coming to dinner.

Well, I'm not old and I like him. Oh, he is so rude! I could have slapped him. And he only looked at me once. He will have a hard time in life, Samuele, unless he learns to be more gracious. Isn't there anybody he likes, no? besides you?

Yes, he's engaged to a girl in the United States.

Dark hair or light?

I don't know.

Mark my words, he will be very unhappy, unless he learns to be more amiable. But think! what intelligence, what an eye! And how wonderful it is to see such an absence of trickery, you know, such simplicity. Does he live here?

No, he just brings his books in here when it's too cold in his own room.

He is poor?

Yes.

He is poor!

Not very poor, you know. When he really gets down to his last cent he can always find things to do at once. He's happy to be poor.

And he lives quite alone?

Yes. Oh, yes.

And he is poor. (This caused her a moment's astonished reflection, until she burst out:) But you know, that is not right! It is society's duty ... that is, society should be proud to protect such people. Someone very gifted should be appointed to watch over such people.

But, Princess, James Blair values his independence above everything. He doesn't want to be watched over.

They should be watched over in spite of themselves. Look, you will bring him to tea some day. I am sure my husband's library has some more old maps of the Campagna. We have the bailiff's reports of the Espoli back into the Sixteenth Century. Wouldn't that bring him?

Even surprised at herself, the Princess tried for a time to talk of other things, but presently she returned to praise what she called Blair's single-mindedness; she meant his self-sufficiency, for while we are in love with a person our knowledge of his weaknesses lies lurking in the back of our minds and our idealization of the loved one is not so much an exaggeration of his excellences as a careful "rationalization" of his defects.

When next I saw Blair he wasted two or three hours before he got up courage to ask me who she was. He listened darkly while I spoke my enthusiasm. At last he showed me a note in which she asked him to drive with her to Espoli, look over the estate, and to examine the archives. He was to bring me if I wanted. James wished greatly to go; but he was suspicious of the lady. He liked her and yet he didn't. He was trying to tell me that he only liked ladies who didn't like him first. He twisted the letter about trying to decide, then going to the table wrote a note of refusal.

Then began what it is merely brutal to call a siege. Driving in the Corso Alix would say to herself: There's nothing unconventional in my stopping at his room to see if he wants to drive in the Gardens. I could do as much for a dozen men and it would be perfectly natural. I am much older than he is, so much so, that it would merely be an act of ... thoughtfulness. When she stood on the platform before his door (for she was not content to send up the chauffeur) she would experience a moment of panic, wishing to recall her ring, imagining when no one answered that he was in hiding behind the closed door, listening, who knows, in anger or contempt to her loud heartbeats. Or she would debate all evening among the gilt chairs of her little salon as to whether she might drop him a note. She would count the days

since last she had spoken to him and gauge the propriety (the inner, the spiritual propriety, not the
worldly propriety: for the Cabalists the latter had
ceased to exist) of a new meeting. She was always
coming upon him by accident in the city (she called
it her proof of the existence of guardian angels) and
it was with these chance meetings that she had generally to content herself. She would attract his attention
the length of the Piazza Venezia and carry him to
whatever destination he confessed to. No one has
ever been happier than Alix on these few occasions
when she sat beside him in her car. How docilely she
sat listening to his lecture; with what tenderness she
secretly noticed his tie and shoes and socks: and with
what intensity she fixed her gaze upon his face trying
to imprint upon her memory the exact proportions of
his features, the imprint that indifference retains so
much better than the most passionate love. There was
a possibility that they might have become the most
congenial of friends, for he dimly sensed that there
was something in her that allied her to the great
ladies of his study. If she had only succeeded in concealing her tenderness. At the first signs of his liking
for her she would become so intoxicated with the inti-
mation of cordiality that she would make some shy
little remark with a faintly sentimental implication;
she would comment on his appearance or ask him to
lunch. And lose him.

One day he gave her a book that had been mentioned in their conversations. He did not stop to think
that it was the first move he had made spontaneously
in the whole relation. Hitherto every suggestion, every invitation, had proceeded from her (from her,
trembling, presuffering a rebuff, lightly) and she
longed for a first sign of his interest. When this book

79

was brought to her, then, she lost her balance; she thought it justified her in pushing the friendship on to new levels, to almost daily meetings, and to long comradely lazy afternoons. She never realized that in his eyes she was, first, an enemy to his studies, and second, that strange hedged monster which all his wide reading had not been able to humanize: a married woman. She called once too often. Suddenly he changed; he became rude and abrupt. When she climbed his stairs he *did* hide behind the door and the bell rang in vain and with a menacing sound, though she had her ways of knowing he was in. She became terrified. Again she confronted that cavern of horror in her nature: she seemed always to be loving those that did not love her. She came to me, distraught. I was cautious and offered her philosophy until I could sound Blair in the matter.

Blair came to me of his own accord. He paced up and down the room, bewildered, revolted, enraged. His stay in Rome had become impossible. He no longer dared remain in his room and when he was out he clung to the side streets. What should he do?

I advised him to leave town.

But how could he? He was in the middle of some work that. Some work that. Damn it all. All right, he'd go.

I begged him before he went to come to dinner with me once when the Princess would be present. No, no. Anything but that. I, in turn, became angry. I analyzed the different kinds of fool he was. An hour later I was saying that the mere fact of being loved so, whether one could return it or not, put one under an obligation. More than an obligation to be merely kind, an obligation to be grateful. Blair did not understand, but consented at last on the difficult condition that I was not to reveal to the Princess that he was leaving for Spain on the very night of the dinner.

Of course, the Princess arrived early, so enchantingly dressed that I fairly floundered in admitting her. She held tickets for the opera; one no longer cared to hear *Salome,* but *Petrushka* was being danced after it, at ten-thirty. Blair's train left at eleven. He arrived and played his most gracious. We were really very happy, all of us, as we sat by the open window, smoking and talking long over Ottima's excellent *zabaglione* and harsh Trasteverine coffee.

It was a continual surprise to me to see that in Blair's presence she was always a proud detached aristocrat. Even her faintly caressing remarks were such as would not be noticed if one had let them fall to someone with whom one was not secretly in love. Her fastidious pride even drove her to exaggerating her impersonality; she teased him, she pretended she did not hear when he addressed her, she pretended she was in love with me. It was only when he was not present that she became humble, even servile; only then could she even imagine calling on him unasked. At last she rose: It's time to go to the Russian Ballet, she said.

Blair excused himself: I'm sorry I must go back and work.

She looked as though a sword had gone through her. But surely, three-quarters of an hour with Stravinsky is a part of your work. My car's right here.

He remained firm. He too had a ticket for that night.

For a moment she looked blank. She had never met obstinacy under such conditions and did not know what to do next. After a moment she bent her head and pushed back her coffee-cup. Very well, she said

81

lightly. If you can't, you can't. Samuele and I shall go.

Their parting was grim. During the drive to the Constanzi she remained silent, fingering the folds of her coat; during the ballet she sat at the back of the box thinking, thinking, thinking, with staring dry eyes. At the close scores of friends pressed about her in the corridor. She became gay: Let's go to the cabaret run by the Russian refugees, she said. At the door of the cabaret she dismissed her chauffeur, telling him that her maid need not sit up for her. We danced for a long time in silence, her depression stealing back upon her.

When we left the hall the unfriendliest moonlight in the world was flooding the street. We found a carriage and started towards her home. But falling into the most earnest conversation in all our acquaintance we failed to notice that the carriage had reached her door and had been standing there for some time.

Look, Samuele, do not make me go to bed now. Let me go in and change my clothes quickly. Then let us drive about and watch the sun come up over the Campagna. Would that make you angry with me?

I assured her that it was just what I wanted and she hurried into the house. I paid off the driver who was drunk and quarrelsome and when she rejoined me we strolled through the streets talking and gradually inviting a resigned drowsiness. We had experimented with vodka at the cabaret and the alcohol conferred upon our minds the same mood that the moonlight was shedding upon the icy bubble of the Pantheon. We strayed into the courtyard of the Cancelleria and criticized the arches. We returned to my rooms for cigarettes.

Last night I wasn't at all brave, she said, lying back

in the darkness on the sofa. I was desperate. That was before I received your invitation. Could I go to see him or couldn't I? A week had gone by. I asked myself would he feel ... well, insulted, if a lady knocked on his door at ten o'clock. It was about ten o'clock. Really, there's nothing peculiar about a lady's paying a perfectly impersonal call at about nine-thirty. There's nothing self-conscious, Samuele, about my being here now, for instance. Besides I had a perfectly good reason for going. He asked me what I thought of *La Villegiatura*, and since then I had read it. Now tell, my dear friend, would it have been ridiculous from the American point of view if I had ... ?

Beautiful Alix, you are never ridiculous. But wasn't your meeting with him tonight all the fresher, all the happier, just because you hadn't seen him for so long?

Oh, how wise you are! she cried. God has sent you to me in my trouble. Come by me and let me hold your hand. Are you ashamed of me when you have seen me suffer so? I suppose I should be ashamed. You see me without any dignity. You have kind eyes and I am not ashamed in front of you. I think you must have loved too, for you take all my foolishness as a matter of course. Oh, my dear Samuele, every now and then the thought comes over me that he despises me. I have all the faults that he hasn't. When I have this nightmare that he not only dislikes me but laughs at me, yes, laughs at me, my heart stops beating and I blush for hours at a time. The only way I can save myself then is by remembering that he has said many kind things to me; that he sent me that book; that he has asked after me. And then I pray God very simply to put into his mind just a bit of re-

gard for me. Just a bit of respect for those things ...
those things that other people seem to like in me.

We sat in silence for a time, her feverish hand
plunged deep into mine and her bright eyes gazing
into the darkness. At last she began speaking again in
a lower voice:

He is good. He is reasonable. When I am analytical
this way I unfit myself for his loving me. I must learn
to be simple. Yes. Look, you have done so much for
me, may I ask for one more favor. Play to me. I must
get out of my mind that wonderful music where Petrushka wrestles with himself.

I felt ashamed of playing before her who played
far better than any of us, but I drew out my folios
and started right through Gluck's *Armice*. I had
hoped that the inept performance would awaken an
esthetic annoyance and so shake her out of her dejec-
tion, but I presently saw that she had fallen asleep.
After a long and adroit diminuendo I left the piano,
turned on a shaded light near her, and stole off into
my own room. I changed my clothes and lay down
ready for the walk in which we were to see the sun
rise. I was trembling with a strange happy excitement, made up partly of my love and pity for her,
and partly from the mere experience of eavesdrop-
ping on a beautiful spirit in the last reaches of its
pride and suffering. I was lying thus, proud and
happy in the role of guardian, when my heart suddenly stopped beating. She was weeping in her sleep.
Sighs welled up from the depths of her slumber,
hoarse protests, obstinate denials and moans followed
one upon another. Suddenly her broken breathing
ceased and I knew she was awake. There was a half-
minute of silence; then a low call: Samuele.

Hardly had I appeared at the door before she

cried: I know he despises me. He runs away from me. He thinks me a foolish woman who pursues him. He tells the servant to tell me he is out, but he stands behind the door and hears me go away. What shall I do? I'd better not live. I'd better not live any more. It's best, dear Samuele, that I go out right now, in my own way, and stop all this mistaken, this, this, futile suffering of mine. Do you see?

She had arisen and was groping for her hat. I really have courage enough tonight, she muttered. He is too good and too simple for me to worry him as I do. I'll just slip out . . .

But Alix, I cried. We love you so. So many people love you.

You can't say that people love me. They like to greet me on the stairs. They like to listen and smile. But no one has ever watched under my window. No one has secretly learned what I do every hour of the day. No one has . . .

She lay back on the sofa, her cheeks flushed and wet. I talked to her for a long time. I said that her genius was social, that she was made for the delight of company, that she relieved others of the weight of their own boredom, their disguised self-hatred. I promised her that she could find happiness in the exercise of her gift. I could see by a glimpse of her wet cheek turned away that it calmed her to be told so, for she possessed the one form of genius that is almost never praised to its face. She grew more tranquil. After a pause she began talking in a dreamy tone:

I will leave him alone. I will never see him again, she began. When I was a girl and we lived on the mountains, Samuele, I had a pet goat named Tertullien that I loved very much. One day Tertullien died.

I would not be comforted. I was hateful and obstinate. The nuns with whom I went to school could do nothing with me and when it was my turn to recite I refused to speak. At last my dear Mother Superior called me into her room and at first I was very bad, even with her. But when she began to tell me of her losses I flung my arms about her and wept for the first time. As a punishment she made me stop everyone I met and say to them twice: *God is sufficient! God is sufficient!*

After a pause she added: I know that it can be true for other people, but I still wanted Tertullien. When is your patience with me coming to an end, Samuele?

Never, I said.

The windows were beginning to show the first light of dawn. Suddenly a little bell rang out nearby, a tinkle of purest silver.

Hush, she said. That's the earliest mass at some church.

Santa Maria in Trastevere is just around the corner. Hurry!

We let ourselves out of the palace and breathed the cold gray air. A mist seemed to hang low about the street; puffs of blue smoke lay in the corners. A cat passed us. Shivering but elated we entered the church joining two old women in wadded clothes and a laborer. The basilica loomed above, the candles of our side-chapel picking out reflections in the curious marbles and the gold of the mosaics in the vast black cave. The service of the Mass was enrolled with expedition and accuracy. When we came out a milky light had begun to fill the square. The shutters of several shops were being lowered; drowsy passers-by made the diagonals staggering; a woman was lowering her

86

chickens in a basket from the fifth story for a long day's scratching.

We walked over to the Aventine, crossing the Tiber which twisted like a great yellow rope under a delicate fume. We stopped for a glass of sour blue-black wine and a paper bag of peaches.

For the time at least the Princess seemed to herself to have forever closed her mind to even the remotest hope that she would ever see Blair again. Sitting on a stone bench on the gloomy Aventine while the sun shouldered its way up through plunging orange clouds, we mused. She seemed for a time to have fallen back into her old despondency; I resumed the arguments that spoke more glowingly of her gifts.

Suddenly she straightened up. All right. I will try it for you. I must do something. Where are you going today?

I murmured that Mme. Agaropoulos was giving a sort of a musicale: that she was introducing a young compatriot who claimed to have discovered the secret of ancient Greek music.

Write her a note. Telephone her. Ask her if I may come. I too shall learn about ancient Greek music. I shall be introduced to everyone there. I shall be asked to everyone's house. Listen, Samuele, since you say it is my talent I shall get to know everyone in Rome. I shall die of social engagements: Here lies the woman who never refused an invitation. I shall meet two thousand people in ten days. I shall lay myself out to please anybody on earth. And mind you, Samuele, if that does not nourish me, we shall have to finish trying, you know. . . .

Mme. Agaropoulos was staggered with joy when she discovered that the unhoped for, the improcurable Princess was coming to her house. Mme. Agarop-

87

oulos was not the slave of social categories, but she longed to frequent the Cabala, as some long for the next world. She assumed that in that company all was wit and love and peace. There one would find no silly people, none envious, none quarrelsome. She had met the Princess d'Espoli once and had ever since taken her as the type of person she would herself have been if she had been better-looking, thinner and had had more time to read, little realizing that all these had been more in her power than in Alix', and that she had spoiled her own progress by a lazy kindliness, great kindliness but lazy.

The Princess called for me in her car at five o'clock. It would be impossible for me to describe her clothes; it is enough to say that she had the most incredible power of supplying new angles, shades, lines, that interpreted her character. This aptitude received added éclat from her residence in Italy, for Italian women, though often more beautiful, lack both figure and judgment. They anxiously spend enormous sums in Paris and achieve nothing but bundles of rich stuffs that bulge or trail or blow about them in effects they half guess to be unsuccessful, and seek to repair with a display of stones.

We pursued the Via Po for a mile or two and alighted at the ugliest of its houses, an example of that modern German architecture that has done so much for factories. As we mounted the stairs she kept muttering: Watch me! Watch me! In the hall we found a host of latecomers standing with their fingers on their lip while from the drawing rooms there issued the sound of passionate declamation accompanied by the plucking of a lyre, the desolate *moto perpetuo* of an oriental flute and a rhythmic clapping of hands. In other words we had arrived too early; our campaign for meeting two thousand souls in ten days was being balked at the outset. Fretted we pushed on into the garden behind the house. Sitting down on a stone bench, with the tragic ode still faintly sounding in our ears we gave our attention to the spectacle in the middle distance of a white-haired gentleman in a wheel-chair overflowing with brightly-colored shawls. This was Jean Perraye; I told the Princess of how Mme. Agaropoulos had found the saintly old French poet at the point of death, wrapt in shawls in a wretched little hotel at Pisa, and how by supplying him with tender interest, whole milk and a group of pet animals she had restored his muse, comforted his last years and effected his entrance into the French Academy. At this moment he was engaged in addressing a circle of attentive cats. These six cats, intermittently licking the fine silk of their shoulders, and casting polite glances at their patron, were gray angoras, the color of cigarette ash. We had read the poet's latest book and knew their names: six queens of France. We practically dozed on the bench—the hot sunlight, the choruses of the *Antigone* behind and Jean Perraye's exordium to the queens of France and Persia before, would have made drowsy even those who had not passed a night of confession and tears.

When we came to ourselves the audition was over and the company, doubly noisy after music, was shouting its appreciation. We re-entered the house, hungry for pastry and encounters. A sea of hats, with scores of self-conscious eyes staring about in perpetual search of new salutations, marking down the Princess for their own; occasionally the large stomach of a senator or an ambassador swathed in serge and bound with a golden chain.

Who's the lady in the black hat? whispered Alix.

Signora Daveni, the great engineer's wife.

Fancy! Will you bring her to me or should you take me to her. No, I'll go to her. Take me.

Signora Daveni was a plain little woman presenting the high lifted forehead and fresh eyes of an idealistic boy. Her husband was one of Italy's foremost engineers, an inventor of many tremendous trifles in airplane construction and a bulwark of conservative methods in the rising storm of labor agitation. The Signora was on every philanthropic committee of any importance in the whole country and during the War had directed incalculable labors. The consciousness of her responsibilities combined with a touch of brusqueness from her humble extraction had brought her into many a short triumphant struggle with cabinets and senates and there are stories of her having sharply rebuked the vague, well-intentioned interferences of the royal ladies of Savoy. Yet these distinctions had only made her manners the simpler and her quick cordiality was continually deflating the deference that was paid to her. She dressed badly; she walked badly, her large feet pushing before her like those of some jar-carrier in an upland village. It had been rather fine in uniform, but now that she must return to hats and gowns and rings the consciousness of her lack of grace caused her much depression. Her home was in Turin, but she lived a great deal in Rome out among the open lots of the Via Nomentana and knew everyone. The Princess with the unexpectedness that lies in the very definition of genius turned the conversation upon the use of sphagnum moss as a surgical dressing. The diverse excellence of the two women glimpsed one another; the Princess was astonished to find such quiet mastery in a woman without a *de* and the Signora was amazed to find the same quality in a noblewoman.

I drifted off, but presently the Princess rejoined me. She is real, that woman. I am going to dinner with her Friday; so are you. Find me some more. Who is that blonde with the voice?

You don't want to know her, Princess.

She must be important with that voice; who is she?

She is the woman in the whole world who is most your opposite.

Then I must know her. Will she give me tea and introduce me to a dozen people?

Oh, yes, she'll do that. But you haven't a thing in common. She is a narrow British woman, Princess. Her only interest is in the Protestant Church. She lives in a little British hotel. . . .

But where does she get that *authority*—and the Princess made a gesture of perfect mimicry.

Well, I admitted, she has received the highest honors an Englishwoman can receive. She wrote a hymn and they made her a Dame of the British Empire.

You see I must be caught out of myself. I must meet her right now.

So I led her up to Dame Edith Steuert, Mrs. Edith Foster Prichard Steuert, author of "Far From Thy Ways, I Strayed," the greatest hymn since Newman's. Daughter, wife, sister, what not, of clergymen, she lived in the most exciting currents of Anglicanism. Her conversation ran on vacant livings and promising young men from Shropshire, and on the editorials in the latest *St. George's Banner* and *The Anglican Cry*. She sat on platforms and raised subscriptions and got names. She seemed to be forever surrounded by a ballet of curates and widows who, at her word, rose and swayed and passed the scones. For she was the author of the greatest hymn of modern times and gazing at her one wondered when the mood could have struck this loud conceited woman, the mood that had prompted those eight verses of despair and humility. The hymn could have been written by Cowper, that gentle soul exposed to the flame of an evangelism too hot even for Negroes. For one minute in her troubled girlhood all the intermittent sincerity of generations of clergymen must have combined in her, and late at night, full of dejections she could not understand, she must have committed to her diary that heartbroken confession. Then the fit was over, and over for ever. It was a telling example of that great mystery in religious and artistic experience: the occasional profundity of nobodies. Dame Edith Steuert on being presented, straightened visibly to show that she was not impressed by the title. With a candor that was another surprise, Alix asked her if she might use her name as reference on her nephew's application for entrance into Eton College. To be sure the nephew was in Lyons, but if Dame Edith would permit the Princess to call upon her some afternoon she would bring some of the boy's letters, photographs and sufficient apparatus to convince her that he was a student recommendable. Friday afternoon was agreed upon, and the Princess rejoined me for new introductions.

So it went on for an hour. The Princess had no method; each new encounter was a new problem. Within three minutes the meeting became an acquaintance, and the acquaintance a friendship. Little did the new friends guess how strange it was to her. She kept asking me what their husbands "did." It delighted her to think that their husbands did anything; she had never guessed that one could meet such people and smiled amazedly like a girl about to meet a real printed poet. A doctor's wife, the wife of a man in rubber, fancy.... Toward the end of the afternoon her enthusiasm waned. I feel a little dusty, she whispered. I feel very Bovary. To think that all this has been going on in Rome without my knowing it. I'll go and say goodbye to Mme. Agaropoulos,—*tiens*, who is that beautiful lady. That is an American, isn't it? Quick.

For the only time in my life I saw the beautiful and unhappy Mrs. Darrell who had come to take leave of her Roman friends. As she entered the room a silence fell upon the company; there was something antique, something Plato would have seized upon in the effect of her beauty. She made much of it, with that touch of conceit that we allow to a great musician listening exaggeratedly to his own perfect phrasing, or to the actor who sets aside author, fellow-players and the fable itself, in order to improvise the last excessive moments of a death scene. She dressed, she glanced, she moved and spoke as only uncontested beauties may: she too revived a lost fine art. To this virtuosity of appearing, her illness and suffering had added a quality even she could not estimate, a magic of implied melancholy. But all this perfection of hers was unapproachable; none of her dearest friends, not even Miss Morrow, dared to kiss her. She was like a statue in a solitude. She presuffered her death, and her spirit was set in defiance. She hated every atom of a creation where such things were possible. The next week she was to retire to her villa at Capri with her collection of Mantegnas and Bellinis and to live through four months with their treacherous love-affair and to die. But this day in the serenity of the selfishness that was her perfection and the selfishness that was her illness she effaced the room.

93

He would have loved me if I had looked like that, breathed Alix into my ear, and sinking into a retired chair covered her mouth with her hand.

Mme. Agaropoulos took Helen Darrell's fingertips a little timidly and led her to the finest chair. No one seemed able to say anything. Luigi and Vittorio, sons of the house, went up and kissed her hand; the American ambassador approached to compliment her.

She is beautiful. She is beautiful, muttered Alix to herself. The world is hers. She will never have to suffer as I must. She is beautiful.

It would not have consoled the Princess if I had explained to her that Helen Darrell, having been admired extravagantly from the cradle, had never been obliged to cultivate her intelligence to retain her friends and that, if I may say it respectfully, her mind was still that of a school-girl.

Fortunately the flautist was still there to play and during the performance of the Paradise music from Orpheus scarcely a pair of eyes in the room left the newcomer's face. She sat perfectly straight, allowing herself none of the becoming attitudes which music suggests to her kind, no ardent attention, no starry-eyed revery. I remember thinking she marked too deliberately the anti-sentimental. When the music was over she asked to be taken to say goodbye, for the present, to Jean Perraye. From the window I could see them alone together, with the gray cats, queens of France, moving meaninglessly about them One wonders what they said to one another as she knelt beside his chair: as he said later, they loved one another because they were ill.

Alix d'Espoli would not stir until she knew that Mrs. Darrell had left the house and garden. All her suffering had rushed back upon her. She pretended to be sipping a cup of tea while she gathered herself together. I understand now, she murmured hoarsely. God has never meant me to be happy. Others may be happy with one another. But I shall never be. I know that now. Let us go.

Then began what was ever after known to the Cabala as Alix aux Enfers. She would lunch at a tiny pension with some English spinsters; stop in at some studio in the Via Margutta; pass through a reception at an Embassy; dance till seven at the Hotel Russie as the guest of some cosmetic manufacturer's wife; dine with the Queen Mother; hear the last two acts of the Opera in Marconi's box. Even after that she might feel the need of finishing the day at the Russian cabaret, perhaps contributing herself a monologue to the program. She no longer had any time to see the Cabala and it watched her progress with terror. They begged her to come back to them, but she only laughed at them with her bright febrile eyes and dashed off into her new-found whirlpools. Long after when some Roman name arose in their conversation they would all cry: Alix knows them! To which she would reply coolly: Of course I know them, and a roar would arise from the table. The acquaintances she was now pursuing for distraction, I had long since pursued for study or from simple liking; but she soon outstripped me by the hundreds. I went to a few engagements with her, but often enough we would come upon one another in ludicrous situations; whereupon we would retire behind a door and compare notes as to how we got there. Did Commendatore Boni ask a few people to the Palatine? she was there. Did Benedetto Croce give a private reading of a paper on George Sand? we glimpsed one another gravely in that solemn air. She lost a comb in defense

95

of Reality at the stormy opening of Pirandello's *Sei Personaggi in Cerca d'Autore;* at Casella's party for Mengelberg, who had been surpassing himself at the Augusteo, dear old Bossi stood on her train and the sound of ripping satin caught the enraptured ear of a dozen organists.

When the bourgeoisie discovered that she was accepting invitations there was a tumult as of many waters. Most of her hostesses assumed that she would not have come to them were it not for the fact that better doors were beginning to be closed against her, but fair or foul they would accept her. And they had her at her best; the faint touch of frenzy that was driving her on only rendered her gift the more dazzling. People who had spent their lives laughing at tiresome jokes were now given something to laugh at. She would be begged to do this or that "bit" which had become famous. Have you heard Alix do the Talking Horse? No, but she did the Kronprinz in Frascati for us last Friday. Oh, aren't you lucky!

For the first time she was seeing something of artists and among them she was enjoying her liveliest successes. The underpainting of her misery which especially these days rendered her wit so magical was much clearer to them than to the manufacturers. They never failed to mention it and their love led them to paying her the strangest tributes which at the time she was in too great a daze to stop and value.

For a while I thought she was enjoying all this. She would laugh so naturally over some of the accidents of the days. Moreover I noticed that she was forming some very rare attachments and I hoped that the friendship of Signora Daveni or of Duse or of Besnard would be able to comfort and finally reconcile her. But one evening I was suddenly shown how utterly ineffectual this plunging about the jungle was.

After a month's absence James Blair wrote me from Spain that he had to come back to Rome, even if it were only for a week. He promised to see no one, to keep up side streets and to get out as soon as it was possible.

I wrote him back in the strongest profanity that it was impossible. Go anywhere else. Don't fool with such things.

He replied, no less angry, that he could move about the earth as freely as everybody else. Whether I liked it or not he was coming to Rome the following Wednesday and nothing would stop him. He was on the traces of the Alchemists. He wanted to know all that was left of the old secret societies and his search was leading to Rome. Since I could do nothing to prevent his coming I could at least devote my energies to concealing it. I took almost ridiculous precautions. I even saw to it that Mlle. de Morfontaine had Alix in Tivoli over the week-end and that Besnard had her sitting for a portrait most of the mornings. But there is a certain spiritual law that requires our tragic coincidences. Which of us has not felt it? Take no precautions.

The seer whom Blair had returned to visit, Sareptor Basilis, lived in three rooms on the top floor of an old palace in the Via Fontanella di Borghese. Rumor had it that he could make lightning play about his left hand and that when his meditations approached ecstasy he could be seen sitting among the broken arcs of a dozen rainbows; and that as you mounted the dark stairs you fought your way through the welcoming ghosts as through a swarm of bees. In the front room where the meetings were held (Wednesdays for adepts, Saturdays for beginners) one was awed by discovering a circular hole in the roof that was never closed. Under it had been laid a zinc-lined depression that carried off the rain water and in this depression stood the master's chair.

Long meditation and ecstatic trances had certainly beautified his face. His blue-green eyes, not incapable of sudden acuteness, drifted vaguely about under a smooth pink forehead; he had the bushy white eyebrows and beard of Blake's Creator. Except for his long walks he seemed to have no private life, but sat all day and night under the hole in the roof, lending an ear to a whispering visitor, writing slowly with his left hand, or gazing up into the sky. A host of people from every walk of life sought him out and held him in reverence. He gave no thought to practical necessities, for his admirers, spiritually prompted, were continually leaving significant looking envelopes beside him on the zinc-lined depression. Some left bottles of wine and bars of bread, and brown silk shirts. The only human occupation that arrested his attention was music, and it is said that he would stand by the door of the Augusteo on the afternoon of a symphony concert and wait for some passerby, spiritually prompted, to buy him a ticket. If none came, he would continue on his way without bitterness. He composed music himself, hymns for unaccompanied voices which he affirmed he had heard in dream. They were written in a notation resembling our own, but not sufficiently so to allow of transcription. I have puzzled for hours over the score of a certain *Lo, where the rose of dispersion empurples the dawn.* This motet for ten voices, a chorus of angels on the last day, began plainly enough with the treble clef on five staves, but how was one to interpret a sudden

98

shrinkage of the horizontal lines to two in all parts? I humbly approached the master on this subject. He replied that the effect of the music at that point could only be expressed by a radical departure from standard notation; that the economy of staves denoted an acuity of pitch; that the note on which my thumb was reposing was an E, a violet E, an E of the quality of a lately-warmed amethyst ... music powerless to express ... ah ... the rose of dispersion empurples. At first the nonsense in which he moved and thought enraged me. I invented opportunities for provoking his absurdity. I improvised a story about a pilgrim who had come up to me in the nave of the Lateran and told me it was God's will that I should return with him to a leper colony in Australia. Dear Master, I cried, how shall I know if this be my real vocation? His answer was not clear. I was told that destiny herself was the mother of decision, and that my vocation would be settled by events not by consideration. In the next breath I was bidden to do nothing rashly; to lay my ear over the lute of eternity and to plan my life in harmony with the cosmic overtones. During the course of a year thousands of women visited him, of every rank, and in every sort of perplexity, and to each one he offered the comforts of metaphor. They came away from him with shining faces; these phrases were beautiful and profound to them; they wrote them in their diaries and murmured them over to themselves when they were tired.

Basilis was attended by two homely sisters, the Adolfini girls. Lise must have been thirty and Vanna about twenty-eight. They say that he ran across them in the Italian quarter of London where they were serving as attendants in a ballet school. Penury and abuse had left them scarcely the human semblance.

Every evening at eleven when they had unlaced the last slipper of the night class, treated the floor with tallow, polished the bars and tied up the chandelier, they went around the corner to the Café Roma for a thimbleful of coffee to sip with their bread. Here Basilis was to be found, a photographer's assistant with grandiose pretensions. He was vice-president of the Rosicrucian Mysteries, Soho Chapter, a group of clerks, waiters and idealistic barbers who found compensation for the humiliations they underwent by day in the glories they ascribed to themselves by night. They met in darkened rooms, took oaths with one hand resting on the works of Swedenborg, read papers on the fabrication of gold and its metaphysical implications, and elected one another with great earnestness to the offices of arch-adept and *magister hieraticorum*. They corresponded with similar societies in Birmingham, Paris and Sydney, and sent sums of money to the last of the magi, Orzinda-Mazda of Mount Sinai. Basilis first discovered his power over the minds of women when he fell into the habit of talking to the two mute sisters in the café. They listened wide-eyed to his stories of how some workmen near Rome, breaking by chance into the tomb of Cicero's daughter, Tulliola, discovered an ever-burning lamp suspended in mid-air, its wick feeding on Perpetual Principle; of how Cleopatra's son Caesarion was preserved in a translucent liquid "oil of gold," and could be still seen in an underground shrine at Vienna; and of how Virgil never died, but was alive still on the Island of Patmos, eating the leaves of a peculiar tree. The wonder-stories, the narrator's apocalyptic eyes, the excitement of being spoken to without anger, and the occasional offer of Vermouth bewitched the sisters. They became his unquestioning

100

slaves; with the money they had saved up he opened a Temple where his gift met extraordinary success. The girls left the ballet school and became doorkeepers in the house of their lord. The new leisure into which they entered, the sufficient food, the privilege of serving Basilis, his confidence and his love, combined to constitute a burden of happiness almost too great to be borne. Happiness is in proportion to humility: the humility of the Adolfini girls was so profound that there was in it no room for the expression of gratitude or surprise; in the face of it food could not fatten them nor love soften their bony features; not even when after some altercation with the London police Basilis and his handmaidens removed to their native Rome. To be sure the master in turn never confessed his indebtedness to the girls for their silent and skillful ministration. Even in love he was impersonal; they merely provided him with that mood of gentle satiety of the senses which is an indispensable element of the philosopher's meditation.

It was under this skylight then that Blair and I sat at about eleven-thirty, waiting for the public séance to begin. We were early, and leaning back against the wall we watched the little group of visitors that one by one moved up to the unboxed confessional that was the master's ear. A clerk with watery eyes and trembling hands; a stout lady of the middle class, gripping a large shopping purse and talking with great rapidity about her *nepote;* a trim little professional woman, probably a lady's maid, stuffing a tiny handkerchief into her mouth as she sobbed. Basilis' eyes seldom strayed to his visitors' faces; while he dismissed them with a few measured grave sentences his glance revealed nothing but its serene abstraction. Presently a younger woman, heavily veiled, crossed

101

the floor swiftly to the empty chair beside him. She must have been there before, for she lost no time in greetings. Under deep emotion she pleaded with him. A little surprised by her vehemence he interrupted her several times with the words *Mia figlia*. The reproaches only increased her energy, and brushing back her veil with her hand in order to thrust her face into the sage's she revealed herself as Alix d'Espoli. Terror went through me; I seized Blair's arm and made signs that we were to escape. But at that moment the Princess with a gesture of anger, as though she had come, not so much to ask the sage's counsel, as to announce a determination, rose and turned to the door. Unerringly her eyes met ours, and the rebellious light died out, to be replaced by fear. For a moment the three of us hung suspended on one cord of horror. Then the Princess collected herself long enough to tincture the despairing contraction of her mouth with a smile; she bowed to us deliberately in turn and passed almost majestically from the room.

At once I returned home and wrote her a long letter, using the whole truth as a surgeon in an extremity would resort to a wholesale guesswork with the knife. I never received an answer. And our friendship was over. I had often to meet her again, and we even came finally to have agreeable conversations together, but we never mentioned the affair and there was a glaze of impersonality over her eyes.

From the night she had seen us in Basilis' rooms the Princess gave up her social researches as abruptly as she had begun them. Nor did she ever go to the Rosicrucian again. I heard that she was attempting the few remaining consolations that lie open to affliction: she took to the fine arts; she climbed up ladders respectfully placed for her in the Sistine Chapel and stared at the frescos through magnifying glasses; she resumed the culture of her voice and even sang a little in public. She started off on a trip to Greece, but came back without any explanations a week later. There was a hospital phase during which she cut off her hair and tiptoed about among the wards.

At last the beating of the wings, the darting about the cage, subsided. She had come to the second stage of convalescence: the mental pain that had been so great that it had to be passed into the physical and that expressed itself in movement, had now sufficiently abated to permit her to think. All her vivacity left her and she sat about in her friends' homes listening to their visitors.

Little by little then her old graces began to reappear. First a few wry sarcasms, gently slipping off her tongue; then some rueful narratives in which she appeared in a poor light; then ever so gradually the wit, the energy, and last of all the humor.

The whole Cabala trembled with joy, but pretended to have noticed nothing. Only one night when for the first time at table she had returned to her gorgeous habit of teasing the Cardinal on his Chinese habits, only once on leaving the table did he take her two hands and gaze deep into her eyes with a significant smile that both reproached her for her long absence and welcomed her back. She blushed slightly and kissed the sapphire.

I, who know nothing about such things, assumed that the grand passion was over and dreaded any moment seeing her interesting herself in some new Northerner. But one little incident taught me how deep a wound may be.

One afternoon at the villa in Tivoli we were standing on the balcony overlooking the falls. Whenever she was left alone with me her charm abated; she seemed to be fearing that I might attempt a confidence; the muscles at the corners of her mouth would tighten. We were joined from the house by a well-known Danish archaeologist who began to discourse upon the waterfall and its classical associations. Suddenly he stopped and turning to me, cried:

Oh, I have a message for you. How could I have forgotten that! I met a friend of yours in Paris. A young American named Blair—let me see, was it Blair?

Yes, Doctor.

What a young man! How many of you Americans are like that? I suppose you never met him, Princess? . . .

Yes, replied Alix, I knew him too.

Such intelligence! He is surely the greatest instinctive scholar I have ever met, and, believe me, perhaps he is all the greater for never putting anything down on paper. And such modesty, Princess,—the modesty of the great scholar that knows that all the learning one human head can hold is but a grain of dust. I spent two whole nights over his notebooks and I honestly felt as though I had brushed against a Leonardo, really, a Leonardo.

We both stood rapt, listening to the waves of happy praise when suddenly I became aware that the Princess had fainted beside me with a happy smile upon her face.

BOOK FOUR

---

# ASTRÉE-LUCE AND THE CARDINAL

There was a vague understanding among the members of the Cabala that I was engaged upon the composition of a play about Saint Augustine. None of my friends had ever seen the manuscript (even I was surprised to come upon it every now and then at the bottom of my trunk), but it was treated with enormous respect. Mlle. de Morfontaine especially kept asking about it, kept walking about on tiptoes and glancing at it sideways. It was to this that she was alluding in the note I received soon after Blair's frightened departure: Try and arrange to come up to the Villa for a few weeks. It is perfectly quiet until five o'clock every afternoon. You can work on your poem.

It was my turn for a little peace. I had so recently passed through the desperations of Marcantonio and Alix. I sat holding the note for a long while, my wary nervous system begging me to be cautious, begging me to make sure that no hysterical evenings could possibly lie behind it. Here was a place where it was perfectly quiet until five o'clock every afternoon. It was five o'clock every morning that I wanted to be reassured about. You can work on your poem. Surely the only vexation that could proceed from that wonderful lady lay exactly there,—she would be asking me every morning about the progress on the Third Act. It would be good for me to be hectored about my play. And what wonderful wines she stored. To be sure the lady was mad, indubitably mad. But mad in a nice way, with perfect dignity; decently mad on a million a year. I wrote her I would come.

What could have been more reassuring than the first days? Mornings of sunlight when the dust settled thicker on the olive leaves; when the terraced hillside seemed to be powdering away; when no sound reached the garden but the cry of a carter in the road, the cooing of doves, stepping high along the eaves of the gardener's shed, and the sound of the waterfall with its mysterious retardations, a sound of bronze. I ate luncheon alone under a grape arbor. The rest of the day was spent in roaming over the hills or among the high chairs of Astrée-Luce's rich and curious library.

From the middle of the afternoon one sensed the approach of dinner. One felt the gradual tightening of the chord of formality until, like the bursting of some pyrotechnical bomb, full of dazzling lights and fascinating detail, the ceremony began. For hours there had come a hum as of bees from the wing of the house that contained the kitchen; there followed the flights of maids and hairdressers through the corridors, the candle-lighter, the flower-bearers. The crushing of gravel under the window announces the arrival of the first guests. The majordomo clasps on his golden chain and takes his place with the footmen at the door. Mlle. de Morfontaine descends from her tower kicking her train about to teach it its flexibility. A string quartet on the balcony begins a waltz by Glazounov as subdued as a surreptitious rehearsal. The evening takes on the air of a pageant by Reinhardt. One passes to the saloon. At the head of the table behind peaks of fruits and ferns, or cascades of crystal and flowers, sits the hostess, generally in yellow satin, her high ugly face lit with its half-mad surprise. She generally supports a headdress of branching feathers and looks like nothing so much as a bird of the Andes blown to that bleakness by the coldest Pacific breezes.

I have described how Miss Grier brooded over her table and placed herself to hear every word whispered by her remotest guest. Astrée-Luce followed a contrary procedure and heard so little of what was said that her very guest of honor was often obliged to resign all hope of engaging her attention. She would seem to have been caught up into a trance; her eyes would be fixed on some corner of the ceiling as though she were trying to catch the distant slamming of a door. Generally some Cabalist held the opposite end of the table: Mme. Bernstein, huddled up in her rich fur cape, looking like an ailing chimpanzee and turning from side to side the encouraging amiability of her grimace; or the Duchess d'Aquilanera, a portrait by Moroni, her dress a little spotty, her face a little smudged, but somehow evoking all the passionate dishonest splendid barons of her line; or Alix d'Espoli making passes with her exquisite hands and transforming the guests into witty and lovable and enthusiastic souls. Miss Grier seldom came, having festivals of her own to direct. Nor was it often

107

possible to invite the Cardinal, since any company to meet him must be chosen with infinite discretion.

Almost every evening after the last guest had left the hill or retired to bed, and the last servant had finished finding little things to adjust, Astrée-Luce and I would descend into the library and have long talks over a drop of *fine*. It was then that I began to understand the woman and to see where my first judgments had been wrong. This was not a silly spinster of vast wealth nourishing a Royalist chimaera; nor the sentimental half-wit of the philanthropic committees; but a Second-Century Christian. A shy religious girl so little attached to the things about her that she might awake any day and discover that she had forgotten her name and address.

Astrée-Luce has always illustrated for me the futility of goodness without intelligence. The dear creature lived in a mist of real piety; her mind never drifted long from the contemplation of her creator; her every impulse was goodness itself: but she had no brains. Her charities were immense but undigested; she was the prey of anyone who wrote her a letter. Fortunately her donations were small, for she lacked the awareness to be either avaricious or prodigal. I think she would have been very happy as a servant; she would have understood the role, have seen beauty in it, and if her position had been full of humiliation and trials it would have deeply nourished her. Sainthood is impossible without obstacles and she never could find any. She had heard over and over again of the sins of pride and doubt and anger, but never having felt even the faintest twinge she had passed through the earlier stages of the spiritual life in utter bewilderment. She felt sure that she was a wicked sinful woman, but did not know how to go about her own reform. Sloth? She had been on her knees an hour every morning before her maid appeared. So difficult, so difficult is the process of making oneself good. Pride? At last after intense self-examination she thought she had isolated in herself some vestiges of pride. She attacked them with fury. She forced herself to do appalling things in public in order to uproot the propensity. Pride of appearance or of wealth? She soiled her sleeves and bodice intentionally and suffered the silent consternation of her friends.

She read the lessons so literally that I have seen her give away her coat time after time. I have seen her walk miles with a friend who asked her to go as far as the road. Now I was to learn that her fits of abstraction were withdrawals into herself for prayer and adoration, and often caused by almost ludicrous incidents. I was no longer left to wonder why all references to fish and fishing sent her off into the clouds; I realized that the Greek word for fish was the monogram of her Lord and acted upon her much as a muezzin's call acts upon a Mohammedan. A traveller spoke flippantly of the pelican; at once Mlle. de Morfontaine repaired to her mental altar and besought its guest not to grieve at the disrespect paid to one of His most vivid symbols. Strangest illustration of all was shown me a little later. One day she chanced to notice on my hall table an envelope which I had addressed to Miss Irene H. Spencer, a teacher of Latin in the High Schools at Grand Rapids, who had come over to put her hand on the Forum. At once Astrée-Luce insisted on meeting her. I never told Miss Spencer why she had been tendered so amazing a luncheon, why her hostess had listened so breathlessly to her trivial travelogues, nor why on the fol-

109

lowing day a golden chain hung with sapphires had been left at the pension for her. In fact Miss Spencer was a devout Methodist and would have been shocked to learn that IHS meant anything.

Strange though Mlle. de Morfontaine was, she was never ridiculous. Such utter refusal of self can by sheer excess become a substitute for intelligence. Certainly she was able to let fall remarkably penetrating judgments, judgments that proceeded from the intuition without passing through the confused corridors of our reason. Though she was exasperating at times, at others she would abound in almost miraculous perceptions of one's needs. People as diverse as Donna Leda and myself had to love her, one moment almost with condescension as to an unreasonable child, and the next with awe, with fear in the presence of something of infinite possibility. Whom were we entertaining unawares? Might this, oh literally! be an . . . ?

This then was the being whom I came to know during those late conversations in the library over a drop of *fine*. The talk was leisurely, full of pauses and to no point, but my bruised instinct could no longer escape the conviction that there was some deeply important matter that she wished to submit to me. I soon foresaw that I was not to rest. My dread of the revelation however was heightened by the obvious difficulty Astrée-Luce found in coming to the point. Finally instead of trying to avoid the discussion I tried to provoke it; I thought I could help here and there by opening veins of conversation that might surprise her problem. But no. The happy moment hung off.

One evening, she asked me abruptly whether it would greatly interfere with my work if we were to move to Anzio for a few days. I replied that I should like nothing better. All I knew of Anzio was that it was one of the resorts on the sea, a few hours from Rome, the site of one of Cicero's villas, and near Nettuno. She added a little anxiously that we should have to go to a hotel, a very poor hotel at that, but that it was out of season and there were ways in which she could supply some of the deficiencies of the service. A little foresight could prevent my being too uncomfortable.

So one morning we climbed into the large plain car she reserved for travelling and drove westward. The back seat served as a warehouse. One glimpsed a maid, a prie-dieu, a cat, a real panel by Fra Angelico, a box of wines, fifty books and some window curtains. I found out later that there had been a lavish assortment of caviare, pâté, truffles and ingredients for rare sauces by which, with a discouraging failure to understand me, she intended to supplement the resources of a tourists' hotel. She drove, herself, and in nothing did Heaven's interest in her reveal itself more clearly. First we stopped at Ostia so that I might see the veritable spot where the last scene of my wretched play took place. We read aloud the page of Augustine and I silently vowed to renounce forever any notion of rephrasing it.

On our first evening at Anzio a cold wind blew in from the sea. The vines and shrubs whipped the houses; the lamps of the cafés about the square swung cheerlessly over wet tables; one could not escape the desolate slip-slap of the waves against the sea-wall. But we both had a taste for such weather. We decided at about six o'clock to walk to Nettuno returning for dinner at half-past nine. We wrapped ourselves in rubber and started off, leaning against the wind and spray and feeling strangely exhilarated.

For a time we walked in silence, but entering at last that portion of the road that lies between the high walls of the villas, Astrée-Luce began to talk:

I have told you before, Samuele (the whole Cabala had followed the Princess in calling me Samuele), that the hope of my life is to see a king reigning in France. How impossible such a thing seems now! No one knows it better than I. But everything I love most is improbable. And it is the fact that it seems so untimely that will help us most when we come to prepare the Divine Right of Kings as a dogma of the Church. What anger there will be, what sneers! Even important churchmen will rush down to Rome and beg us not to upset the progress of Catholicism by such a move. There will be controversies. All the newspapers and the reviews will be shouting and weeping and laughing and the whole basis of democratic government, the folly of republics, will be aired. Europe will be cleansed of the poison in its side. We have nothing to fear from debates. The people will turn to God and ask to be ruled by those houses of His choosing. —However, I am not trying to convince you of it now, Samuele; I am only stating it so as to lead up to something else. You are a Protestant; does this make you impatient? Are you tired of me?

No, no, please. I am very interested, I replied.

At that moment our road brought us again to the water's edge. We stood for a moment on a parapet looking down on the loud sea that plunged about on the washing stones of a village. It began to rain. Astrée-Luce was gripping the iron railing watching the steam that rose from the waves; she was crying silently.

Perhaps, she continued, as we returned to our journey, you can imagine the tenth part of my disap-

112

pointment as I watch the Cardinal getting older, and myself, and the nations falling deeper and deeper into error, and so little done. He can help us. He seems to me to have been especially created to help us. I do not forget his work in China. It was heroic. But what a greater work remains for him in Europe. Year follows year and still he sits up there on the Janiculum, reading and walking in the garden. Europe is dying. He will not stir.

At the time I was deeply moved. The rain and her tears and the puddles and the slapping noises of the water against the seawall had begun to affect me. All the voices of nature kept repeating: Europe is Dying. I would have liked to stop and have a good meaningless cry myself, but I had to listen to the voice beside me:

I cannot understand why he does not write. Perhaps I am not meant to understand. I know he believes that the universality of the Church is imminent. I know that he believes that a Catholic Crown is the only possible rule. But he does not stir to help us. All we ask from him is a book on the Church and the States. Think, Samuele, his learning, his logic, his style—but you have never heard him preach? His irony in controversy and his amazing perorations! What would be left of Bosanquet? The constitutions of the republics of the world would be tossed about—you will forgive me if I seem disrespectful to your great country—tossed about like eggshells. His book would not be just a book fallen from the press: it would be a force of nature; it would be the simultaneous birth of an idea in a thousand minds. It would be placed at once in the canon and bound up with the Bible. And yet he spends his day among rose bushes and rabbits and reading histories of this and that. I want to do this in my lifetime, I want to arouse this great man to his task. And you can help me.

I was excited. The air was full of a divine absurdity. Here was someone who was not afraid of using superlatives. This was being mad on a great scale. It would be hard to come down to ordinary living after these intoxicating threats against the presidents of this world and the binderies of the British Bible Society. I tried to think of something to say. I mumbled something about willingness.

She did not notice my inadequacy. It seems to me, she continued, that I have at last discovered one of the causes of his reluctance to join us. But first, tell me how he is regarded by the various Romans whom you have met. What is his legend among people who do not know him?

Here I was frightened. Could *she* have heard? How could any of those strange rumors have reached her?

But she would learn nothing from me. I took leave of good faith and told her all the favorable reports I had heard. Simple souls were captivated by the thought that apart from a few major obligations he lived on sixty-five lire a week; that he spoke twelve languages; that he enjoyed polenta; that he visited in certain Roman homes (her own, in particular) without ceremony; that he was translating the Confessions and the Imitation into exquisite Chinese. I knew Romans who so loved the very thought of him that they took walks to the Janiculan Hill solely to peer between his garden gates and lurked about the house in the hope of giving their children an opportunity to kiss his ring.

Astrée-Luce waited in silence. At last she said with only a trace of reproach:

You are trying to spare me, Samuele. But I know. There are other stories about him. His enemies have been at work systematically poisoning his prestige. We know that there is no one in Rome who is kinder, more humble, higher-minded; but among the common people he has almost the reputation of a monster. Some people have been at work spreading such rumors deliberately. And the Cardinal has heard of them: through the whispering of servants or by cries in the road, or by anonymous letters, in all sorts of ways. He exaggerates this attitude. He feels that he is in a hostile world. It has made his old age tragic. And that is why he will not write. Yet it is within our power to save him still.—But look! There is a franco-bollo shop. Let us get some cigarettes and find some place to sit down. It makes me so happy to talk of this!

Provided with cigarettes we looked about for a wine shop. Our wish evoked one at the next curve in the road, a smoky uncordial tunnel, but we sat down before the glasses of sour inky wine and continued our conspiracy. Astrée-Luce confessed that if the ill-odor had become attached to the Cardinal's name through any real delinquencies on his part, we could not have hoped to dissipate it. Truth in such subtle regions as rumor would be unalterable. But she knew that the aspersions in this case were the result of a clever campaign and she felt sure that a countercampaign could still sweeten his reputation. In the first place our enemies had taken advantage of the Italians' prejudice against the Orient. An Italian enjoys the same delicious shudder at the sight of a China-man that an American boy does at the mention of a trapdoor over a river. The Cardinal had returned from the East yellow, unwrinkled. His walk troubled

115

them. It was easy to build upon this, to pass the whisper along the Trasteverine underworld that he kept strange images, that animals (his gardenful of rabbits and ducks and guinea fowl) could be heard shrieking late at night, that his faithful Chinese servant had been seen in all sorts of terrifying attitudes. Next, his frugal life stirred their imaginations. Every one knew he was fabulously wealthy. Rubies as big as your fist and sapphires like doorknobs, where were they? Did you ever go up to the gate of the Villino Wei Ho? Come with me Sunday. If you sniff hard enough you can get the strangest odor, one that will leave you drowsy for days and give you dreams.

We were to change all this. We sat there choosing a committee of rehabilitation. We were to have magazine articles, newspaper paragraphs. His eightieth birthday was approaching. There would be presentations. Mlle. de Morfontaine was donating a Raphael altar piece to his titular church. But most of all we would send out agents among the people telling them of his goodness, his simplicity, his donations to their hospitals, and ever so faintly his sympathy with socialistic ideas; he was to be the People's Cardinal. We had anecdotes of his snubbing the arrogant members of the College, of his defending a poor man who had stolen a chalice from his church. China was to be re-created for the Trasteverines. And so on. We were to prop up the Cardinal so that the Cardinal could prop up Europe.

When we returned to the hotel that night Astrée-Luce seemed to have grown ten years younger. Apparently I was the first person to whom she had outlined her vision. She was so eager to be at work that she suddenly asked me if I minded packing up again and going back to Tivoli that night. We could the

116

better start work in the morning. What she really wanted was the exhilaration and fatigue of driving (her terrible driving) before she went to bed. So we put back into the car the maid, the Fra Angelico, the ingredients for sauces and the cat, and returned to the Villa Horace at about two in the morning.

The Cardinal was not to know that we were putting up a scaffolding about his good name and freshening the colours; but we were to persuade him not to do some of the things that particularly antagonized the public. The very next morning Astrée-Luce shyly begged me to go and see him. She did not know why, but she had a vague idea that now I knew her hopes my eyes would be open to significant details.

I found him as one could find him every sunny day the year round, seated in the garden, a book on his knee, a reading glass in his left hand, a pen in his right, a head of cabbage and a Belgian hare at his feet. A pile of volumes lay on the table beside him: *Appearance and Reality,* Spengler, *The Golden Bough, Ulysses,* Proust, Freud. Already their margins had begun to exhibit the spidery notations in green ink that indicated a closeness of attention that would embarrass all but the greatest authors.

He laid aside his magnifying glass as I came up the path of shells. *Eccolo, questo figliolo di Vitman, di Poe, di Vilson, di Guglielmo James,—di Emerson, che dico!* What do you want?

Mlle. de Morfontaine wants you to come to dinner Friday night, just the three of us.

Very good. Very nice. What else?

What do you want, Father, for your birthday? Mlle. de Morfontaine wants me to sound you tactfully . . .

Tactfully!—Samuelino, walk to the back of the

117

house and tell my sister you will stay to lunch. I am to have a little Chinese vegetable dish. Will you have that or a little risotto and chestnut-paste? You can buy yourself something solid on the way down hill. How is Astrée-Luce?

Very well.

A little illness would be good for her. I am uncomfortable when I am with her. There are certain doctors, Samuele, who are not happy when they are talking to people in good health. They are so used to the supplicating eyes of patients that say: Shall I live? In the same way I am ill at ease in the company of persons who have never suffered. Astrée-Luce has eyes of blue porcelain. She has a fair pure heart. It is sweet to be in the company of a fair pure heart, but what can one say to it?

There was St. Francis, Father . . . ?

But he had been libertine in his youth, or thought he had.—Senta! Who can understand religion unless he has sinned? who can understand literature unless he has suffered? who can understand love unless he has loved without response? *Ecco!* The first sign of Astrée-Luce's being in trouble was last month. There is a certain Monsignore who wants her millions for his churches in Bavaria. Every few days he climbs the hill to Tivoli and breathes into her ear: *And the rich He hath sent empty away.* The poor child trembles and pretty soon Bavaria will have some enormous churches, too ugly for words. Oh, you know, there is for every human being one text in the Bible that can shake him, just as every building has a musical note that can overthrow it. I will not tell you mine, but do you want to know Leda d'Aquilanera's? She is a great hater, and they say that during the Pater Noster she closes her teeth tight upon: *Sicut et nos dimittimus debitoribus nostris.*

At this he laughed for a long time, his body shaking in silence.

But was not Astrée-Luce devoted to her mother? I asked.

No, she has had no losses. That was when she was ten. She has poetized her, that is all.

Father, why did not that literal faith of hers carry her to a convent?

She promised her dying mother she would stay alive to put a Bourbon on the throne of France.

How can you laugh, Father, at her devotion to ...

We old men are allowed to laugh at things that you little students may not even smile about. Oh, oh, the house of Bourbon. Would you be surprised if I gave up my life to reviving the royal brother-and-sister marriages of Egypt? Well! It is not more impossible.

Dear Father, won't you write one more book? Look, you have about you all the greatest books of the first quarter of my century ...

And very stupid they are, too.

Won't you make us one. Such a great book, Father Vaini. About yourself, essays like Montaigne,—about China and about your animals and Augustine ...

Stop! No! Stop at once. You frighten me. Do not you see that the first sign of childhood in me will be the crazy notion that I should write a book? Yes, I could write a book better than this ordure that your age has offered us (and with a sharp blow he pushed over the tower of books; the Belgian hare gave a squeal as he barely escaped being pinned under Schweitzer's *Skizze*). But a Montaigne, a Machiavelli ...a...a...Swift, I will never be. How horrible, how horrible it would be if you should come here some

119

day and find me writing. God preserve me from the
last folly. Oh, Samuele, Samuelino, how bad of you to
come here this morning, and awaken all the vulgar
prides in an old peasant. No, don't pick them up. Let
the animals soil them. What is the matter with this
Twentieth Century of yours . . . ? You want me to
compliment you because you have broken the atom
and bent light? Well, I do, I do.—You may tell our
rich friends, tactfully, that I want for my birthday a
small Chinese rug now reposing in the window of a
shop on the Corso. It would be unbecoming for me to
say more than that it is on the left as you approach
the Popolo.—The floor of my bedroom is getting
colder every morning, and I always promised myself
that when I became eighty I might have a rug in my
bedroom.

What went wrong?
The first hour was delightful. The Cardinal always
ate very little (never meat) and that with preposter-
ous slowness. If his soup took him ten minutes his
rice required half an hour. To be sure the elements of
trouble were present merely in these friends' characters. They were so different that just to hear them
talking together had an air of high comedy. First,
Astrée-Luce made the mistake of referring to the Ba-
varian Monsignore. She suspected that the Cardinal
was out of sympathy with any plans she might have
of helping the Church in that direction; she longed to
talk over with him the problem of her wealth and its
disposition, but he refused to give her the least advice. He had endless resources of ingenuity in evad-
ing the subject. As Rome was arranged at that time it
was most important that he should exercise no influence on that aspect of his friend's life. Yet he allowed

it to be seen that he knew she would handle the matter foolishly. It ailed him to see such an enormous instrument for progress drift down the wind of ecclesiastical administration.

Now we must remember that it was the eve of his eightieth birthday. We have already seen that the event had precipitated a flood of amused bitterness. As he said later, he should have died at the moment of leaving his work in China. The eight years that had elapsed since then had been a dream of increasing confusion. Living is fighting and away from the field the most frightening changes were taking place in his mind. Faith is fighting, and now that he was no longer fighting he couldn't find his faith anywhere. This vast reading was doing something to him. . . . But most of all we must remember his terror at the thought that the people of Rome hated him. He would leave in dying a memory without affection and without dignity. An anonymous letter had told him that even in Naples children were kept in good behavior with threats that the Yellow Cardinal would skin them. If one were young one would laugh at such a rumor, but being old one grew cold. He was leaving a world where he was shuddered at for a world that was no longer as distinct as it had been, but which might yet have this consolation that he would not be able to look down from it and see the people surreptitiously spitting on the endings in *issimus* that would compose his epitaph.

Before I knew it we were in the middle of a wrangle about prayer. Astrée-Luce had always longed to hear the Cardinal discourse upon abstract matters. She had often tried to draw him into arguments on the frequent communion and on the invocation of the saints. He had once whispered to me that she was

121

trying to extract from him the materials for a calendar, such sweet manuals as she could buy in the Place Saint Sulpice. Every word of his was sacred. She would not have hesitated to put him in a Church window with St. Paul. It was only after a few moments that she became aware that he was saying some rather strange things. Could that be Doctrine? If anything he said was difficult all she had to do was to try hard to grasp it. Truth, new truth. So she listened, first with surprise, then with mounting terror.

He was launched upon the paradox that in prayer one should never ask for anything. His dialectic was doing an incredible work. He had decided to be Socratic and was asking Astrée-Luce questions. He wrecked her on several orthodox assumptions. Twice she fell into heresy and was condemned by the councils. She seized hold of St. Paul but the epistle broke in her hand. She came to the surface for the third time but was struck by a Thomist fragment. The previous week the Cardinal had been called to the deathbed of a certain Donna Matilda della Vigna, and it was poor Donna Matilda who was now dragged forth to point the argument. Exactly what had the survivors been praying for? Astrée-Luce was easily routed from the more obvious positions. She became frightened. Presently she rose:

I don't understand. I don't understand. You are joking, Father. Aren't you ashamed of saying such things to bewilder me, when you know how I value everything you say.

Look, then, continued the Cardinal. I shall ask Samuele about this. As he is only a Protestant it will be very easy to entangle him. Samuele, may I assume that God may have intended Donna Matilda to die before long anyway?

Yes, Father, for she died that very night.

But we thought that if we prayed very sincerely we might change His mind.

Why ... there is authority for our hoping that in extremities our prayer may. . . .

But she died. Then we were not sincere enough! Or persevering enough! Good! Sometimes He grants and sometimes He doesn't, and Christians are expected to pray hard on the chance that this is one of the times He might relent. What a notion! Astrée-Luce, what a thought!

Father, I can't stay and hear you talk this way ...

What a view of these things. Listen. It is incredible that He should change His mind. Because we frightened mortals are on the carpet? Oh! You are a slave to the idea of bargain. The money changers are still in the temple!

Here Astrée-Luce, gone quite white, returned to the arena with one more brave venture: But, Father, you know He answers the requests of a good Catholic. Then she added in a lower voice with tears in her eyes. But you were there, dear Father. If you had deeply wished it you could have altered the ...

Here he half rose from his chair crying with terrible eyes: Insane child! What are you saying? I? *Have I no losses?*

Now she flung herself upon the floor before him. You have been saying these things to prove me. What is the answer? I will not let you go until you tell me. Dear Father, you know that prayer is answered. But your clever questions have upset all my old ... old ... What is the answer?

Come, sit down, my daughter, and tell me yourself. Think!

This went on for another half-hour. I grew more

123

and more astonished. Mere prayer as a problem was soon left far behind. It was the idea of a benignant power behind the world that was being questioned now. For the Cardinal it was an exercise in rhetoric, sharpened by his temperamental scepticism on the one hand and by his latent resentment against Astrée-Luce on the other. It was a kind of questioning that would have had no effect on sound intellectual believers. It was disastrous for Astrée-Luce because she was a woman without a reason who just this once was trying to reason. She would so have liked to have been a deep thinker, and when she fell it was through her desire to be a different person.

It went on and on. At every fresh proposal he would now cry Bargain! A Bargain! and point out that her prayers sprang from fear or the greed for comfort. Astrée-Luce was going to pieces. I moved over behind her chair and pleaded with the Cardinal by gesture. Was he tormenting her out of caprice? Did he realize her devotion to himself?

At last she seemed to have a light:

My head is in a whirl. But I know now what you mean me to answer. We may not ask for things, or people, or relief from sickness, but we may ask for spiritual qualities; for instance for the advancement of the Church . . . ?

Vanity! Vanity! How many years have we been praying for a certain good thing? What have statistics shown us?—I refer to the conversion of France.

With a cry Astrée-Luce rose and left the room. I took upon myself to protest to him.

She is foolish, Samuelino. You cannot call those convictions deep that were overturned with straws. No, trust me. This is for her good. I have been a confessor too long to go astray here. She has the spiritual notions of a school-girl. She must be fed on some harsher bread. Understand that she has never suffered. She is good. She is devout. But as I told you the other day, just by accident she has never known trouble.

Just the same, Eminence, I know her well enough to know that this very moment she is in her chapel, clinging to the altar-rails. She will be depressed for weeks.

But just at that moment Astrée-Luce returned. Her manner was agitated and artificially gracious. Will you excuse me if I go to bed now? she asked. (She never called him Father again.) Please stay and talk with Samuele.

No, no. I must be going. But before I go let me tell you·one thing. The real truths are difficult. At first they are forbidding. But they are worth all the others.

I shall be thinking over what we have said.—I . . . I . . . Excuse me, if I ask you something?

Yes, my child, what is it?

Promise me you weren't joking.

I wasn't joking at all.

Did I really hear you say that the prayers of good men are of no . . . ? However. Goodnight. You will forgive my slipping away now?

So they took their leaves.

I went to bed worried. I was worrying about Astrée-Luce. Was she going to lose her faith? What do bystanders do in such a case? The loss of one's faith is always comic to outsiders, especially when the loser is in fine health, wealth, and a fairly sound mind. The loss of any one or all of these has a sort of grandeur; Astrée-Luce should have the loss of her faith depend on one of the others. It's not a thing one loses in fine weather.

I was wakened from a troubled sleep by a discreet

but continuous knocking upon my door. It was Alviero, the majordomo.

Madame says will you please dress and come to her in the library, please.

What's the matter, Alviero?

I do not know, Signorino. Madame have not slept all night. She have been in the church hitting the floor.

All right, Alviero, I'll be there in a minute. What time is it?

Three o'clock and one-half, Signorino.

I dressed rapidly and hurried to the library. Astrée-Luce was still in her gown. Her face was white and drawn; her hair was disheveled. She came toward me with both hands extended: You will forgive my sending for you, won't you? I want you to help me. Tell me: were you made unhappy by the strange things Cardinal Vaini said after dinner?

Yes.

Have you Protestants ideas on these things?

Oh, yes, Mlle. de Morfontaine.

Were his ideas new? Is that what everyone is thinking?

No.

Oh, Samuele, what has happened to me! I have sinned. I have sinned the sin of doubt. Shall I ever have peace again? Can the Lord take me back after I have had such thoughts? Of course, of course, I believe that my prayers are answered, but I have lost ... the ... the reason why I believe it. Surely, there is a key here. Perhaps it's just one word. All you have to do is find the one little argument that makes the whole thing natural. Isn't it strange! I've been looking here (and she pointed at the table which was covered with open books, the Bible, Pascal, the Imitation) but

I don't seem to be able to put my finger on the right place. Sit down and try and tell me, my dear friend, what arguments there are that God hears us speak and will answer us.

I talked to her for quite a long while, but achieved nothing. Perhaps I even made it worse. I told her that I was sure that she still believed. I showed her that the very fact that she was distressed about it proved that she was furiously believing. After an hour of this wrestling she seemed a little comforted, however, and picking up a fur coat went back to her cold chapel and prayed diligently for faith until the morning.

At about ten she appeared in the garden and asked me to read a note that she was sending to the Cardinal. I was to pass on it. Dear Cardinal Vaini, I will always honor you above all my friends. I think you love me and wish me well. But in your great learning and multiple interests you have forgotten that we who are not brilliant must cling to our childhood beliefs as best we may. I have been inexpressibly troubled since yesterday evening. I want to ask a favor of you: that you indulge my weakness to the extent of not touching upon matters of belief when I am with you. It gives me great pain to have to ask you this. I beg of you to understand it as apart from any personal feelings of unfriendliness. I hope that I may grow strong enough to talk of these matters with you again.

It was a very bad letter, but that was perhaps due to the content. I suggested shyly that she omit the last sentence. So she copied it and sent it off by a special messenger.

Soon the day came for the end of my stay in the Villa. She came up to my room for a last talk.

Samuele, you have been with me during the sad-

127

dest days of my life. I cannot deny that all interest has gone out of living for me. I still believe, but I don't believe as I used to. Perhaps it was not right that I went through life as I did. Now I know that I rose up every morning full of unspeakable happiness. It seldom left me. I had never thought before that my beliefs in themselves were unbelievable. I used to boast that they were, but I did not know what I was saying. Now hours come to me when I hear a voice saying: There is no prayer. There is no God. There are people and trees, millions of them both, every moment dying.—You will come and see me again, won't you, Samuele? Have I made it very unpleasant for you in the house?

When I reached my rooms in Rome I found three letters from the Cardinal asking me to come and see him at once. As I entered the gate he came toward me eagerly:

How is she? Is she well?

No, Father, she is in great trouble.

Come inside, my son. I must speak to you.

When we entered his study, he closed his door behind him, and said with great emotion: I want to say to you that I have sinned, greatly sinned. I cannot rest until I have tried to repair the harm I have done. Look, look at this letter she has written me.

Yes, I have seen it.

Her letter forbids my explaining what I meant. Is there no way I can reassure her?

There is only one way now. You must regain all her confidence before you touch on such matters again. You must come and go about her house as though nothing had happened—

Oh, but she will never ask me again!

Yes, she is having you all to dinner quite soon, Alix, Donna Leda, and M. Bogard.

Thanks be to God! I thank Thee, I thank Thee, I thank Thee, I thank Thee . . .

May I speak quite boldly, Eminence?

Yes. I am a poor old man, all mistakes. Speak to me as you like.

If you go, take great care not to let slip any remark on religious matters. I beg of you, do *not* try to reinstate yourself with some orthodox comments. She might misunderstand one little word and think you were attacking her faith again. It is very serious. Your ideas are not orthodox, Father, and if you said an orthodox thing it would not sound sincere and that would be worst of all. But if you come and go simply and affectionately, she will lose her horror of you—

Horror of me!

Yes, and very gradually, perhaps after a year, you may be able—

But I may not live a year!

*Es muss sein!*

This struck him as humorous and ruefully he sang Beethoven's phrase, adding: All the avenues of life lead to that.

*Es muss sein.* I should have stayed in China. (Here he fell silent for a while, heaving deep sighs and staring at his yellow hands.) God has chosen to take away my reason. I am an idiot, falling into every ditch. Oh, that I had died long ago—and yet I cannot die until I have righted myself. Hand me that red book behind you. There are two plays about old men, Samuelino, that grow dearer every day to an old man. There is your Lear, and—and opening *Oedipus at Colonus* he translated slowly:

Generous son of Aegeus, to the gods alone old age and death come never. But all else is confounded by all-mastering time. The strength of earth decays and the strength of the body. Faith dies. Distrust is born. Among friends the same spirit does not last true ... and bowing his head he let the book fall to the floor. *Es muss sein.*

I did not go to that dinner. I dined alone with Miss Grier in the city, but at about ten we drove out to Tivoli to sit with the company. As we went I outlined to her discreetly the relations that now existed between two of her best friends: Oh, how stupid he is, she cried. How cruel! What a lot he has forgotten. Don't you see that the whole thing rests, not on the abstract question as to whether her prayers may be answered, but on the question as to whether ONE prayer may be answered? Her prayer for France ... Doesn't he believe such things are real to other people?

He thinks that a little doubt will be good for her. He describes her as the woman who has never suffered.

He is in his dotage. I am so angry I am ill.

At this moment our car drew aside to let pass another hurrying by towards Rome. This was Mlle. de

Morfontaine's great ugly travelling car and the Cardinal was in it.

There he is now, cried Miss Grier. They must have broken up early.

Something's happened, I said.

Yes, something has very likely happened, God forgive us. If everything were all right, Alix would be driving back with him. Our wonderful company is dissolving. Alix no longer trusts us. Leda is losing her good old commonsense. Astrée-Luce has quarrelled with the Cardinal. I'd better leave Rome and go back to Greenwich.

As we approached the Villa we became aware that something indeed must have happened. The front door was open. The servants were gathered in the hall whispering in front of the closed doors of the drawing rooms. As we entered these opened and Alix, Donna Leda and Mme. Bernstein appeared supporting a sobbing Astrée-Luce. They led her up the stairs to her tower. Miss Grier without questioning the servants as to what had happened, gently urged them to return to their rooms. We passed into the drawing room just in time to see M. Bogard leaving by another door and looking considerably shaken. We sat down in silence, our thoughts full of foreboding. Simultaneously we became aware of a faint odor of powder and smoke and glancing about my eye fell upon a rent near the ceiling beneath which a little pile of white dust had collected on the floor. Mme. Bernstein hurried in and after closing the door carefully behind her, came toward us:

Not a soul must hear of this. Oh, this must be kept so quiet. What a thing to happen! Anything is possible after this. What a blessing that no servants were in the room when ...

131

Miss Grier asked her several times what had happened.

I know nothing. I can hardly believe my own senses, she cried. Astrée-Luce must have gone mad. Elizabeth, will you believe me when I tell you that we were sitting here quietly over our coffee—Look, look! I didn't see that hole in the ceiling before!—Isn't it all frightful?

Please, Anna, please tell us what happened!

I am.—There we were sitting over our coffee, talking in low voices of this and that, when suddenly Astrée-Luce went over to the piano, picked up a revolver from among the flowers and shot at the good Cardinal.

Anna! is he hurt?

No. It didn't even come near him. But what a thing to happen! What on earth could have made her do such a 'thing! We were friends—we were all such good friends. I do not understand anything.

Try and think, Anna: did she say anything when she fired at him, or before she fired?

That's the strangest of all. You won't believe me. She called out: The Devil is here. The Devil has come into this room. At the Cardinal!

What had he been saying?

Nothing! Merely everyday things. We had been telling stories about the peasants. He had been telling us about some peasants he had come across on his walks outside S. Pancrazio.

Suddenly Alix appeared: Elizabeth, go to her quickly. She wants to see you. She is alone.

Miss Grier hurried out.

Alix turned to me:

Samuele, you know the majordomo better than we do. Will you go and tell him that Astrée-Luce has

132

had a nervous breakdown. That she thought she saw a burglar at the window, and that she fired at him. It is so important for the dear Father's sake that no hint of this gets about.

I went out and found Alviero. He knew the explanation was insufficient, but utterly devoted to the whole Cabala he could be trusted to dress the story at exactly the points that would most convince the other servants.

Alix did not understand what lay back of the shot, but she was able to recall the conversation that had led up to it. The Cardinal had told the following simple story, an incident he had witnessed in one of his walks outside the city wall:

A farmer wished to break his six-year-old daughter of crying. One afternoon he led her by the hand to the center of a marshy waste, thickly grown with wiry reeds well above the child's head. There he had suddenly flung away her hand, saying: Now are you going to cry any more? The child, with a last rush of contrary pride and with a beginning of fear, started to cry. All right, shouted the father, we don't want any bad children in our house. I'm going to leave you here with the tigers. Goodbye. And jumping out of the child's sight, repaired to a wine shop at the edge of the waste and sat down for an hour's cardplaying. The child strayed about from hummock to hummock, wailing. In due time the father reappeared and taking her affectionately by the hand led her home.

That was all.

But Astrée-Luce had never learned, as the rest of us have, to harden her heart slightly before stories of cruelty or injustice. She may have had no losses of her own, but she had always been ready to expose

133

her imagination to the full force of other people's
wrongs. Such an anecdote would have drawn from
others a sigh, a swift protective contraction of the lips
and a smile of gratitude for its safe conclusion. But to
Astrée-Luce it was the vividest reminder that the God
whose business it was to brood over the world minis-
tering to the discouraged and the mistreated, was no
more. The Cardinal had killed him. There was no one
left to soothe the horse that has been beaten to death.
The kittens that the boys fling against the wall have
no one to speak for them. The dog in torment that
keeps his eyes upon her face, and licks her hands
even while his eyes grow dim, shall have no comfort-
er but her. This was not a casual story the Cardinal
was telling: it concealed a covert allusion to their
conversation of the preceding week. It was a taunt. It
was a sort of curse. Look at the world without God,
he was saying. Get used to it. If she had lost God, oh
how clearly she had gained the Devil. Here he was
triumphing in this lacerating story. Astrée-Luce went
over to the piano, picked up a revolver from the flowers and shot at the Cardinal, crying: The Devil has
come into this room!

As the Cardinal drove back that night he kept repeating to himself the words: Then these things are
real! It had required Astrée-Luce's shot to show him
that belief had long since become for him a delecta-
ble game. One piled syllogism on syllogism, but the
foundations were diaphanous. He strained to remember what faith was like when he had had it. He kept
dragging before his mind's eye the young priest in
China exhorting the families of the Mandarins. That
was himself. Oh, to retrace the way. He would go

134

back to China. If he could look again on the faces that were serene with a serenity he had given them, perhaps he could steal it back. But side by side with this hope was a terrible knowledge: no words could describe the conviction with which he saw himself guilty of the greatest of all sins. Murder was child's play compared to what he had done.

The firing of the shot had done as much for Astrée-Luce. On awaking, her terror lest she had harmed him, later her fear that she had fallen out of reach of his forgiveness was greater than had been her misery in a world without faith. It was given to me to carry from each to the other the first messages of anxious affection. When Astrée-Luce and the Cardinal discovered that they were living in a world where such things could be forgiven, that no actions were too complicated but that love could understand, or dismiss them, on that day they began their lives all over again. This reconciliation was never put into words, in fact it remained to the end merely in a state of hope. They longed to see one another again, but it would have been impossible. They dreamed of one of those long conversations that one never has on earth, but which one projects so easily at midnight, alone and wise; words are not rich enough nor kisses sufficiently compelling to repair all our havoc.

He received permission to return to China, and sailed within a few weeks. Several days after leaving Aden he fell ill of a fever and knew that he was to die. He called the Captain and the ship's doctor to him and told them that if they buried him at sea they would have to face the indignation of the Church, but that they would be fulfilling his dearest wish. He took what measures he could to shift upon himself the blame for such an irregularity. Better, better to be tossing in the tides of the Bengal Sea and to be nosed by a passing shark, than to lie, a sinner of sinners, under a marble tomb with the inevitable *insignis pietate*, the inescapable *ornatissimus*.

---

# BOOK FIVE

# THE DUSK OF THE GODS

When my time came to leave Rome I set aside several days for the last offices of piety, piety in the Roman sense. I wrote a note to Elizabeth Grier arranging for a long late talk on the eve of my departure. There are some questions I want to ask you, I said, which no one can answer. Then I went to the Villino Wei Ho and sat for an hour with the Cardinal's sister. The guinea fowl were less vocal than formerly and the rabbits were still hobbling about the garden looking for a gleam of violet. I went to Tivoli and peered through the iron gates of the Villa Horace. Already it looked as though no one had lived there for years. Mlle. de Morfontaine had returned to her estates in France and was living in the closest retirement. They said that she opened no letters, but I wrote her a note of farewell. I even spent an afternoon in the stifling rooms of the Palazzo Aquilanera, where Donna Leda imparted to me in great confidence the news of her daughter's engagement. Apparently the young man was unable to produce any cousins from among the draughty courts of Europe; his family was merely Italian; but he owned a modern palace. At last a bathroom was to make its appearance in the house of Aquilanera. How time flies!

My most considerable observance was a trip to Marcantonio's grave. I found it by the village cemetery near the Villa Colonna-Stiavelli. Consecrated ground had been denied the boy, but in her bewilderment and love the mother had contrived a false wall of stones and briars that seemed to include his grave among those of souls that the Church felt safe in recommending at the Judgment Day. Here I sat down and prepared to think about him. I was perhaps the only person in the world who understood what had brought him there. The last office of friendship would be to think about him. But some birds were singing; a man and his wife were cultivating the ground in the next field; the sunlight was heavy. Hard as I tried I could not keep my thoughts on my friend; it was not difficult to recall his features or to meditate about dissipation; but really elegiac reflection escaped me, Marcantonio. I drove back to Rome ashamed of myself. But it had been a delightful day in the country, unforgettable June weather.

There was one association I could not renew; I could not go to see Alix. Whenever I met her by chance the barrier of her lowered eyelids told me that we would never have long talks again.

Closing the apartment was melancholy enough. Ottima and I spent hours in packing, our heads bent over our boxes and full of our imminent farewells. She was going back to her wine-shop at the corner.

Long before I bought a ticket she had begun to pray for those in peril on the sea and to notice the windy days. After an exhausting struggle with myself I decided to give her the police dog. Kurt's affections were equally divided between us; in Europe or in America he would pine for an absent friend. Ottima and Kurt would grow old together in a life filled with exquisite mutual attentions. I could swear that before I went to the hotel on that last night Kurt knew I was taking leave of him. There was a grandeur I fell short of in the way he faced an inevitable situation. He placed one paw on my knee and looked to the right and left in deep embarrassment. Then lying down he placed his muzzle between his paws and barked twice.

I found Elizabeth Grier at midnight sitting in the library that Blair had catalogued. Her small neat head looked tired and after some desultory conversation I made a move to go. She reminded me that I had intended asking her some questions.

My questions are harder to put than to answer.

Try.

Miss Grier, did you know that you and your friends were called the Cabala?

Yes, of course.

I shall never know such a company again. And yet there seems to be some last secret about you that I've never been able to seize. Haven't you anything to tell me that will show me what you all meant, how you found one another, and what made you so different from anyone else?

Miss Grier took a few minutes off to think this over. She sat smiling strangely and stroking with her fingertips the roots of her hair beside her left temple. Yes, she said, but it will only make you angry if I tell you. Besides it's very long.

It's not long, Miss Grier, but you will insist on making it long because you hate to have your guests leave before dawn. However, I shall listen to you for hours if you promise to throw some light on the Cabala and the dinners at the Villa Horace.

Well, first you must know, Samuele, that the gods of antiquity did not die with the arrival of Christianity.—What are you smiling at?

You're adorable. You have resolved to make your explanation last forever. I asked about the Cardinal and you have gone back to Jupiter. What became of the gods of antiquity?

Naturally when they began to lose worshipers they began to lose some of their divine attributes. They even found themselves able to die if they wanted to. But when one of them died his godhead was passed on to someone else; no sooner is Saturn dead than some man somewhere feels a new personality descending upon him like a strait-jacket, do you see?

Now, Miss Grier!

I told you it would make you angry.

You don't pretend this is true?

I won't tell you whether this is true, or an allegory, or just nonsense.—Next, I am going to read you a strange document that came into my hands. It was written by a certain Hollander who became the god Mercury in 1912. Will you listen?

Has it anything to do with the Cabala?

Yes. And with you. For I sometimes think that you are the new god Mercury. Take some of that claret and listen quietly.

I was born in a Dutch parsonage in 1885. I was the despair of my home and the terror of the village, a little liar and thief in the full enjoyment of my health and wit. My real life began one morning of my twenty-seventh year when I experienced the first of a series of violent pains in the center of my head. This was my deification. Some untender hand was emptying the cup of my skull of its silly gray brains and filling it with the divine gas of instinct. My body too had its part in this; each microscopic cell had to be transformed; I was not to fall sick or grow old or die, save when I chose. As historian of the gods I have to keep record of an accident whereby, through some monstrosity in spiritual law, an Apollo of the Seventeenth Century failed to completely deify: one arm remained corruptible.

It was then that I discovered the first great attribute of our nature, namely that to wish for a thing is to command it. It does not suddenly fall into your hand or descend in a rosy mist upon your carpet. But circumstances start a discreet ballet about you and the desired thing comes your way through the neatest possible imitation of natural law and probability. Scientists will tell you that they have never seen the sequence of cause and effect interrupted at the instance of prayer or of divine reward or retribution. Do they think, the fools, that their powers of observation are cleverer than the devices of a god? The poor laws of cause and effect are so often set aside that they may be said to be the merest approximations. I am not merely a god but a planet and I speak of things I know. So I stole my mother's savings from under her pillow and went to Paris.

But it is at Rome that we were last worshiped under

our own names, and it is thither that we are irresistibly
called. During the journey I gradually discovered
further traits of my new being. I woke up mornings
to discover that bits of information had been de-
posited in my mind overnight, the enviable knowledge for instance, that I had the power of "sinning"
without remorse. I entered the Porta del Popolo one
midnight in June, 1912. I ran the length of the Corso,
leapt the fence that surrounds the Forum, and flung
myself upon the ruins of my temple. All night in the
fine rain I tore my clothes in joy and anguish, while
up the valley came an interminable and ghostly pro-
cession singing my hymns and hiding me in a tower
of incense. With the coming of dawn my worshipers
vanished and wings no longer fluttered at my heels.
I climbed out of the sunken ruins and went out into
the misty streets in search of some coffee.

Godlike I never reflect; all my actions arrive of
themselves. If I pause to think I fall into error. During the next year I made a great deal of money on
the races at Parioli. I speculated in motion pictures
and African wheat. I went into journalism and the
misrepresentations I sowed will have deferred Europe's recovery from the War many scores of years. I
love discord among gods and men. I have always
been happy. I am the happiest of the gods.

I had been called to Rome to serve as the gods'
messenger and secretary, but more than a year had
passed before I recognized even one. The Church of
Santa Maria sopra Minerva is built over an ancient
temple to that goddess and there one day I found
her. So impatient was I to discover the others that I
disobeyed the laws of my nature and went hunting
for them. I spent hours hanging about the station in

search of newly arrived divinities. One night I strode the platform waiting for the Paris Express. I was trembling with premonition. I had donned a silk hat and its complements, a coral camellia, and a little blonde moustache. Plumed with blue smoke and uttering splendid cries the train rushed into the station. The travelers descended from their compartments into a sea of *fachini* and relatives. I bowed to a Scandinavian diplomat and a Wagnerian prima donna. They returned my greeting hesitantly; a glance into their eyes showed me that they were brilliant but not supernatural. There was no incipient Bacchus among the Oxford students on vacation; the Belgian nuns on pilgrimage discovered me no Vesta. I scanned faces for half an hour until the length of pavement was deserted and a long line of old women with pails appeared. I stopped by the engine to ask a guard if another section of the train was to follow. I turned to see a strange face looking at me from the small window of the locomotive—mis-shapen, black with coal-dust, gleaming with perspiration and content, and grinning from ear to ear, was Vulcan.

Here Miss Grier raised her head: There follow fifty pages describing his encounters with the others. Have you anything to say? Do you recognize anything?

But, Miss Grier, I've had no headaches! I don't receive what I want!

No?

What am I to understand? You've made it twice as confused. Explain some more.

He goes on to say that the gods were afraid of being laughed at for what they had lost. Flight, for instance, and invisibility, and omniscience and free-

143

dom from care. People would forget that they still had a few enviable powers: their strange elation; their command over matter; their ability to live or die when they chose and to live beyond good and evil. And so on.

What became of him?

Finally he decided to die, as they all do. All gods and heroes are by nature the enemies of Christianity—a faith trailing its aspirations and remorses and in whose presence every man is a failure. Only a broken will can enter the Kingdom of Heaven. Finally tired out with the cult of themselves they give in. They go over. They renounce themselves.

I was astonished at the desolation in her voice. It held me back from eagerly demanding of her the application to the Cabala of all these principles. We went into the next room where her musicians were waiting to offer us some English madrigals. The applications still occur to me, especially when I am depressed. They give in. They go over.

On the night that my steamer left the bay of Naples I lay sleepless in my deck-chair until morning. Why was I not more reluctant at leaving Europe? How could I lie there repeating the Aeneid and longing for the shelf of Manhattan? It was Virgil's sea that we were crossing; the very stars were his: Arcturus and the showery Hyades, the two Bears and Orion in his harness of gold. All these passed before me in a cloudless sky and in the water, murmuring before a light wind, the sliding constellations were brokenly reflected.

Mercury is not only the messenger of the gods; he is the conductor of the dead as well. If in the least part his powers had fallen to me I should be able to invoke spirits. Perhaps Virgil could read my mood for me, and raising my two palms I said in a low voice (not loud enough to reach the open port-holes behind me):

Prince of poets, Virgil, one of your guests and the last of barbarians invokes you.

For an instant I thought I saw the shimmer of a robe and the reflection of the starlight on the shiny side of a laurel leaf. I pressed my advantage:

*O anima cortese mantovana*, greatest of all Romans, out of the eternity of that limbo to which the Florentine, perhaps wrongly, consigned you, grant me a crumb of time.

Now indeed the shade stood in mid-air just above the hand-rail. The stars were glittering and the water was glittering, and the great shade, picked out in sparks, was glittering furiously. But the image must become clearer. There was one title that might avail more with him than those of poet or Roman.

Oh, greatest spirit of the ancient world and prophet of the new, by that fortunate guess wherein you foretold the coming of Him who will admit you to His mountain, thou first Christian in Europe, speak to me!

Now indeed the gracious spirit became completely visible with pulsations of light, half silver and half gold, and spoke:

Be brief, importunate barbarian. Except for this last salutation wherein you have touched my only pride, I would not delay here. Detain me not from the absorbing games of my peers. Erasmus is in debate with Plato, and Augustine has descended from the hill and sits among us, though the air is gray. Be brief, I pray you, and give heed to your Latin.

At this I realized that I had no definite question to put to my guest. In order to mark time and prolong so uncommon an interview, I engaged him in conversation:

Was I then right, Master, in assuming that Dante was not completely in God's confidence?

Indignation infused a saffron stain into the noble figure in silver-gold: Where, where is he, that soul of vinegar, that chose to assign the souls of the dead more harshly than God? Tell him that though a pagan I too shall see bliss. It is nothing that I must first pay the penalty of ten thousand years. Behold this moment I exhibit the sin of anger; where is *he* in pain for the sin of pride?

I was a little shocked to discover that neither genius nor death removed us beyond the temptation to asperity, but said: Master, have you met the poets of the English tongue that have come into your groves?

Let us be brief, my friend.—One came that had been formerly blind and did me much honor. He spoke a noble Latin. Those that stood by assured me that in his lines mine were not seldom reflected.

Milton was indeed your son. . . .

But before him came another, greater than he, a writer of pieces for a theatre. He was proud and troubled and strode among us unseeing. He made me no salutation. Vanity no longer exists among us, but it is sweet to exchange greetings among the poets.

He knew but little Latin, Master, and perhaps had never read your page. Moreover in life he was neither the enemy nor advocate of grace and being arrived in your region his whole mind may well have been consumed with anxiety as to his eternal residence. Is he among you still?

146

He sits apart, his hand over his eyes, and only raises his head when, in the long green evenings, Casella sings to us, or when on the wind there drifts from Purgatory the chorus that one Palestrina prepares.

Master, I have just spent a year in the city that was your whole life. Am I wrong to leave it?

Let us be brief. This world where Time is, troubles me. My heart has almost started beating again,—what horror! Know, importunate barbarian, that I spent my whole lifetime under a great delusion,—that Rome and the house of Augustus were eternal. Nothing is eternal save Heaven. Romes existed before Rome and when Rome will be a waste there will be Romes after her. Seek out some city that is young. The secret is to make a city, not to rest in it. When you have found one, drink in the illusion that she too is eternal. Nay, I have heard of your city. Its foundations have knocked upon our roof and the towers have cast a shadow across the sandals of the angels. Rome too was great. Oh, in the pride of your city, and when she too begins to produce great men, do not forget mine. When shall I erase from my heart this love of her? I cannot enter Zion until I have forgotten Rome.—Dismiss me now, my friend, I pray thee. These vain emotions have shaken me.... (Suddenly the poet became aware of the Mediterranean:) Oh, beautiful are these waters. Behold! For many years I have almost forgotten the world. Beautiful! Beautiful!—But no! what horror, what pain! Are you still alive? Alive? How can you endure it? All your thoughts are guesses, all your body is shaken with breath, all your senses are infirm, and your mind ever full of the fumes of one passion or another. Oh, what misery to be a man. Hurry and die!

Farewell, Virgil!

The shimmering ghost faded before the stars, and the engines beneath me pounded eagerly toward the new world and the last and greatest of all cities.